TALES FROM THE VAULT

VOLUME II

A STORY SANCTUM ANTHOLOGY

TALES FROM THE VAULT

VOLUME II

A STORY SANCTUM ANTHOLOGY

Story Sanctum
PUBLISHING

Cover image by Krin Van Tatenhove using Photoshop AI.

Cover design and interior formatting by Casselberry Creative Design.

Story Sanctum Publishing.
First Edition.
ISBN: 979-8-9886653-9-7

Table of Contents

Introduction

You have entered into the Story Sanctum vault! Welcome!

Inside these pages, you will find a rich anthology of stories designed to speak to your heart, mind, and soul.

Story Sanctum is a shrine for sacred storytelling. We curate compelling fiction and nonfiction stories with a clear point of view that captures the truth and beauty, sacredness and strangeness, heartbreak, horror, and hope of the human condition.

For us, sacredness transcends any one religion and does not have to be religious at all. Our stories honor the sacredness of life found in the human experience. The viewpoints of the writers are their own, but they give us unique insights into their lives and our shared human experience.

These tales were taken from our vault of fiction and nonfiction stories. They represent some of our favorite stories from the past year. We hope you will enjoy reading them as much as we did.

Enjoy!

Story Sanctum Editors

Jen & Shawn Casselberry
Joel Klepac
Krin Van Tatenhove

NONFICTION

A Meditation of Delight

Jenn Zatopek

On a cold weekday morning in late winter, I meditated imperfectly leading to a wondrous moment of play, the effects of which nestled down into my heart like sweet birdsong. So much of my life's work has been to unravel the dangerous threads of perfectionism woven into my being, the accompanying shame making it hard to discern what only feels real and what's actually true. In the latter half of living, I listen more to Spirit, whose guidance is like the astonishing words of Leonard Cohen: "There's a crack in everything / That's how the light gets in."

I caught a bit of that astonishment on an ordinary Monday morning during my usual habit of dropping into an online meditation after breakfast. Sitting into my lounge chair rather than at my desk, I slipped under a handmade quilt and opened my laptop, seeing my friends pop on screen for the daily sit at the *Center for Mindful Self-Compassion*. Mirjam led us that day, and her warm presence ushered all of us into a place of deep peace and stillness. I still heard her kind voice leading us in meditation when I fell asleep.

***

Now I'd like to add here that I don't recommend sleeping during meditation all the time. Sitting in meditation is about having an alert yet restful state of mind, which creates the ideal conditions for insights to arise. Remaining awake also helps reshape the more primitive parts of the brain that have been formed through trauma, stress, and overwhelm to become settled in peace, calm, and kindness. And meditation (like prayer) is a practice of awakening to the truth of who we are, defined not by the voices of shame and fear, but of a love deeper and more vibrant than anything we have known. But hear this: please don't shame yourself for falling asleep while meditating because in sleep, we dream of higher things that can awaken us to dramatic shifts in consciousness, which is what happened to me next.

***

Even though I usually meditate upright, I leaned back into my chair due to chronic back pain. Drifting off to a light sleep, I felt uplifted, flying through the air and drifting over tall sunny mountains and deep fertile valleys, near the lands of Albuquerque and Caprock Canyons, Taos and the Hill Country near Austin. I dreamt of course, but the experience felt grounding, even as I flew through the air. Out for only twenty minutes, I awakened with a start and waved goodbye to Mirjam and friends online. I flung myself out of the chair, stretching my arms upward and gazing at the faint blue above the barren pin oak tree outside. A realization dawned on me. *I am made to understand this: I am to visit the garden store now.*

Except that I almost didn't make it to the garden store because a litany of worry thoughts surfaced, which I noticed with curiosity. *Shouldn't I go for a walk instead? I only have fifty minutes till my first appointment, and I need to clean the dishes, straighten the rooms, and practice my Spanish first. What about prayer? Don't I need to sit in contemplative silence first? Does meditation count as prayer? What about making sure I read poetry first? Wouldn't it be better if I finished the book on friendship I started last year? What if . . . ?*

I paused and watched my mind generate reminders of my to-do list, but this time, instead of obeying the worry thoughts, I did the opposite: I drove to the garden store with determination, marveling at the ultramarine sky and the pleasant drive through quiet suburban neighborhoods, past the old Methodist church and over the bridge spanning the river that runs through our city. Everything was bathed in the warmth of a mid-morning sun, the landscape brightened in beauty, my heart peaceful as I drove on.

When I arrived, I parked my car and walked slowly reverently through the store, admiring the red miniature roses, yellow pansies, and fragrant alyssum. I meandered to the small pots of thyme, basil, lavender, oregano, and chives, the leftover herbs from last year's season. Picking up the tiny herb containers, I smiled, remembering all the fun I'd had gardening and the ensuing delight I'd have this year once we begin again. Rather than feeling pressure to buy anything, what arose within me was deep gratitude for the life growing all around us, for the workers who cared for the plants, for the beautiful earth who mothers us every season with the goodness of new growth, the glory of life in simply being.

As I drove home, I was elated because I listened to a voice inside rooted in love and followed an invitation to play. At lunch, I shared the moment with my partner who celebrated my experience, noting it was indeed play, an unstructured time of enjoyment and simply doing with no pressure to perform. *How much life have I lost in striving to be perfect in all things? How much grief do I carry from these moments which are lost to the oblivion of time?* I know when my striving for perfectionism started, how it shaped me for decades to come, but now it doesn't have to define my future. The rest of the day passed in a joyful dance, of feeling light and free as I let go of shame and lived in the moment, my counseling sessions and time with my people a sheer wonder and delight.

***

Why bother sharing these small moments of goodness that come wrapped up in our daily existence? The words of T.S. Eliot come to mind in our fast-paced modern age: "Where is the Life we have lost in living? Where is the wisdom we have lost in knowledge? Where is the knowledge we have lost in information?" I share this moment of play with you now so you can play with the ideas I've presented, pausing at moments where you're offered something different from your usual routine, a sacred opening which could perhaps free you from a familiar path of striving, neural nets driving you to endless work and worry with no payout except more anxiety.

We play and frolic at parks, sing and dance with abandon, laugh our heads off at our friends' jokes, because we know this truth in our bones: there is a better way to live than endless striving and relentless fear. We matter and our play, the forgotten realm of childhood, lives on in our minds, and with great courage and curiosity, we can rise to these moments with an open heart. I'll see you at the garden store near the roses or meet you at the church basement for dancing. Maybe we'll meet at the strange coffeehouse near downtown and have decaf espresso and play that new game together. In any case, I'll know you by that look of joy on your face. We'll laugh and take great care in living, our lives touched by the transcendent beauty of this moment together, this oneness alive right here and right now.

Jenn Zatopek is a writer and trauma-informed psychotherapist living in Texas. A native Texan with New England roots, Jenn writes at the intersection of science and faith, longing to encounter the divine in the most unexpected places. Her work has been featured in *Ruminate Magazine, Fathom*, and elsewhere. More at Jenn's theholyabsurd.com follow her on Instagram.

The World Turns

Susan Evans

Using Granny's ancient knife—the handle worn thin and the blade sharp as a razor—I sliced big ruby tomatoes. Drops of red juice and seeds dribbled onto JFG mayonnaise spread over white bread slices.

Betty and I balanced paper plates and cold Tupperware glasses in our arms, carefully stepped out the back screen door, and headed to an old card table set up under the cool shade of black cherry trees.

Dressed in Mama's 1950's netted hats and faded print dresses, we nibbled our sandwiches and sipped grape Kool aid.

Birds sang in the tree tops, and dark blood-red fruit dangled in small beaded clusters. Juicy tomato seeds slid down our arms, and wet rings of sweaty glasses spotted the table. We pushed up trailing dress cuffs.

Sheltered by leafy boughs, I presided over luncheon, slipping into the role of soap opera society matron as easily as the old musty dress flowed over my thin shoulders.

Hazy images flickered through my mind of plots and subplots I'd watched on the black and white RCA, as Mama ran an iron over our daddy's work clothes: Bert's drunken husband's latest dark act, her daughter-in-law's cheating ways, the light-haired son's gambling problem, and her friend Mata's hush-hush brush with cancer.

All this electric drama, we swallowed as innocently as we did our sandwiches and Kool aid, accepting stories whole, lamenting and shaking our heads at the folly of that grownup, messed up world.

For a few more years, we remained unaware that adulthood edged ever closer, as we tasted the sweet fruit of each year's harvest, covered by a safe canopy of trees and wrapped safely in simple, gauzy dreams.

Too soon, the savor of August tomatoes faded, as did yesterday's summer pretending. The winters came. Gone was our shady corner, as quickly gone as the half-hours of Mama's soap opera. Our young selves became exiled from under the sheltering cherry trees, and our innocent inward turning slowly turned outward with forced change. We -- unable to make-believe anymore -- died to ourselves and thrust into unrehearsed roles in a bewildering world of grownup. Our eyes opened to deep sorrows that could not be resolved by simple black and white stories.

And then one spring a soft easterly breeze came up and blew from the cherry trees a shower of frothy pink masses of blossoms. Hope -- the last vestige of our dreamy childhood -- floated down, too, and we caught hold of it and held on.

After a few more cycles of seasons, we grew strong enough to spin our own stories. They are bittersweet -- unlike those fragrant August tomatoes -- but clearer and wiser than the soap operas ever were. We continue to write and rewrite our lines until they feel right in our mouths; we grow into characters that feel right in our bones.

The black cherry trees died years and years ago, their beauty vanished as the past always does, but my sister's life and mine remain like slender, pale green branches reaching ever for the sun through sometimes dark shade and watery clouds.

Susan H. Evans lives in Baltimore, Maryland, and is published in *Daily Inspired Living Magazine, Journey of the Heart, Glint Journal, Avant Appalachia,* and *Pensive Journal.*

Crab Soup

Christine Brooks

Had it not been for Covid-19 forcing everyone inside, I'm not sure my plan would have worked but looking back, I'm glad I acted on that little nudge from the Universe that said, *this will be fun, let's do it.* It was a time of thoughts and prayers, heartbreak and heartache, and we were resentful that we had to endure any of it.

It was the worst of times. The only consolation offered, if consolations were offered at all, was that we got to endure it together.

Dad was proudly from the South. He was from a small town along the Chesapeake Bay that no one ever heard of. He met my mother while stationed at a nearby air force base, and after the war, he returned to another small town, this time in Massachusetts.

Dad thought nothing of his giant belt buckles, cowboy boots, and handlebar mustache. Over the years his Southern drawl began to fade, against his will, so he took on a twangy

New England accent instead, a sort of Southern fusion.

When Covid-19 hit I was grateful that we lived together, both learning how to start over, him after mom died and me after a difficult breakup. Together we processed our grief and learned to find even the tiniest bits of happiness in life's small offerings.

We spent the first months of being shuttered in learning about the many different birds that enjoyed our feeders and the various types of flowers that grew along the fence but eventually, the weather turned from warm to cool to cold, and even with heavy coats and blankets, we were forced to retreat back inside.

The bungalow-style house was lovely. Its bones held every wonderful memory I had ever experienced. It was small. Not small in a suffocating way though, but small, like a hug.

It was a time of nothing at all and everything at once but at least football was on. Dad watched and cheered for the Patriots and the Irish, but we both knew he would rather be down the street at his American Legion than stuck in the house watching spectator-less football. Still, he never complained and never rolled his eyes when out of sheer boredom I added team after team to our watchlist.

Texas, sure. Good colors. The Seahawks, sure we like Pete Carroll. Titans, yes. Boston College, obviously. Game by game I could find a reason to like a team until finally, we watched every game televised.

During one of the games between two teams that we had grown to dislike for no good reason, Dad sat up in his recliner, slapped his hands on his lap, and announced, "Let's cook."

I loved to cook but after months of being stuck in the house, I truly believed I had made everything possible. I had no new meals to prepare. No new meal options to try. I was convinced I had reached the end of recipes as we knew them. There simply were no more.

Slowly, he got up, shuffled out of the room heading towards his bedroom and after some small commotion, he emerged with a large hardcover book.

"I've been reading," he proudly announced.

"At night? In bed?" I laughed out loud.

Dad could fix anything, build anything, and knew more about the workings of a Whirlpool washing machine than anyone should, but he could not cook and he did not read.

"Here, take a look," he said, shoving the yellow and white hard-covered book in my direction. "I got it off the Amazon."

Still laughing, I pursed my lips together to keep from bursting into a full fit of hysteria.

"So, you've been reading this?" I asked, still shocked by his admission. "I've never seen this book," I said sitting down at the dining room table.

"I had it under my mattress," he said, sitting beside me.

"Why?" I burst out laughing, snorting and all. The image of him pulling a book out from under his mattress, reading by flashlight was just too much.

"I use my flashlight," he said proudly.

"Dad!" I laughed and smiled and snorted again.

Although his room was down the hall from mine, he thought if I noticed his light on late at night, I would think something was wrong.

"I didn't want the light to bother you," he nodded at me. "What do you think? Think we could make some of these?" he asked, hopefully at me for confirmation.

Still laughing and stunned, I looked at the cover, *The Gift of Southern Cooking* by Edna Lewis and Scott Peacock.

"Sure," I said, flipping it open to the section titled, *Praise the lard and pass the biscuits*. The heavy glossy pages contained recipes, pictures, and stories about the ingredients and locale.

"Oh good," he said, pushing his chair closer to mine, "Look, I made some notes," he said, pointing to page 36 and the recipe for She-Crab Soup. "Can we try this one first?"

He was positively giddy now and it was contagious. Excited at the idea of something new, recipes with ingredients I never cooked with before, and doing all this with my father, almost felt indulgent at a time when the world was hurting.

"Can we eat in the garage?" he asked, as nervous as a child asking to stay up past their bedtime on a Sunday night.

Most families did not eat in their garage. Most did not have a full-size stove, refrigerator, and wood stove in their garage and most people did not consider a party in the garage a fun idea, but we were not most people.

Many of our celebrations occurred in the garage. Engagements happened, birth announcements were made, football games, Red Sox baseball, and just about any reason we could think of to consecrate big doin's was a good enough reason to have a "splash" as Dad liked to call them.

At one of the last garage gatherings, Mom announced matter-of-factly that this would be her last "splash." As we sat around, enjoying chips, dip, and various cocktails, Mom said, hand on hips:

"I wanna have a party. I've never had one just for me," she said ready to fight anyone who may suggest that she would be too tired for a said splash.

Pancreatic cancer was an unwelcome guest but one that was determined to have a seat at our table, elbowing its way between the bread and butter.

We cooked on the stove, oven, grill, and deep fryer. Even the wood stove had a pot bubbling with someone's offering.

We held on to the day long past the afternoon shadows that crept over the house, the sounds of children playing hide and seek, and everyone's bedtime. We held on, held each other, and then let go.

When Mom died a few weeks later we locked the garage door, something that we had never done before, and went inside. We thought if we never opened the garage door again, never tossed out *his* beer bottle, never put away *her* sweater, and never hung up *my* baseball hat none of it happened. With the door shut, it was easy to believe that she was just on the other side, still laughing and reminiscing.

"Yes," I smiled. "Let's eat in the garage."

Together, we scanned the glossy-paged book for our first meal. After much debate and scouring the cabinets for ingredients, we decided on crab soup —which did not come as much of a surprise to either of us. Crab legs were on the menu for every special celebration we ever had.

One morning, when I was out walking, Dad unlocked the garage, opened the small sliding window to let the cool December air in, began wiping down the counters, and the stove, and delicately moved her champagne glass to the counter. He gently moved the fluff he found under a couch cushion that held a small family of mice to the safety of a nest he made for them under the grand American yellowwood tree in the yard.

In the familiar whir and buzz of movement in the garage, we felt alive again. We knew it was not a time to celebrate but maybe if we were quiet and respectful, we could have this one small moment of "normalcy."

We worked in harmony, unpacking grocery bags, and stacking up the ingredients on the counter for our Saturday afternoon lunch: four cans of lump crab, rice flour, cayenne pepper, and a bottle of Harvey's Bristol Cream Sherry.

We would start cooking after your nap. You were suddenly tired and had a little headache.

***

I sprinkled in Old Bay seasoning even though the recipe

didn't call for it because you would have insisted on its addition. I used meat from female crabs (mostly) which are fattier and better for soup and whose orange roe gives a distinctive taste, or so the recipe claims.

It smells good, you would say if the dead could talk.

"Pull up a chair," I insist.

But, you cannot. You are in the next room now with Mom listening to Johnny Cash and laughing with the others.

As I touch the wooden spoon to my lips, I can hear your muffled voice telling everyone about our recipe for happiness and the day we almost made She-Crab Soup.

Christine Brooks holds her M.F.A. from Bay Path University in Creative Nonfiction. She has four books of poetry available, *The Cigar Box Poems*, *Beyond the Paneling*, *Inside the Pale*, and *the hook-switch goodbye*. Her debut novel, *TamboMan*, was released in August 2022.

Ash Wednesday, 2017

Richard Brynteson

The Lord is my shepherd; I shall not want.

Ellen and I counted 13 muskrats as we walked around Lake Bennett that late February mild afternoon. Spring had emerged early in Minnesota and the ice had pulled away from the shore, leaving strips of water for the diving and swimming pleasure of these little critters. My wife Ellen worried that they, especially the wee ones, might freeze with the inevitable onslaught of more doses of winter, and die before their time.

He maketh me to lie down in green pastures: he leadeth me beside the still waters.

A week later, on a bike ride at Playa Linda, Mexico, Ellen collapsed with a heart attack in a small, filthy bathroom. I carried her out onto the cement slab, lay her down where a nurse and the bike tour guide tried to pump life back into her.

"Come back," I yelled. I looked around. The gathered onlookers surrounded us. The cement floor pulsated with the heat of the day. The restaurant tables were left unused. Quiet. The nurse took my arm.

"She's gone, Richard."

"She cannot be. She promised me 25 more years."

"She's gone, Richard."

The blasting midday light. The heat. Ellen lying there and dozens watched, gawking. She is not a zoo animal, I wanted to yell. The yellow police tape. This is not the way it was supposed to end. We were supposed to grow old together.

"Go to the light, Ellen. Your Daddy will be there." I sat with her, holding her hand, stroking her arm. I removed her wedding ring and put it on my gold chain with my cross.

He restoreth my soul: he leadeth me in the paths of righteousness for his name's sake.

The ceiling fan spun listlessly, barely dulling the late afternoon heat. An air conditioning unit groaned ineffectively. The beige walls of the Zihuatanejo Police Station, which had not been painted in decades, were spattered with dead flies. The three white plastic chairs and two steel desks were nicked, dented, and scuffed. Danny, the young bike tour guide, relayed his version of Ellen's death to the recorder. The grumpy police chief stomped through the room importantly. The recorder sat behind a desk dutifully, typing the deposition into a large ancient desktop computer. For four long hot hours, we took turns giving our versions of Ellen's death. Later in the evening, the autopsy report cleared me as a suspect. Heart attack. The red mark on her forehead was from falling, which I knew, but they didn't.

Yea, though I walk through the valley of the shadow of death, I will fear no evil: for thou art with me; thy rod and thy staff they comfort me.

It was not Ellen at all, the person who lay, gussied up in lace and white ruffles, in the coffin at the funeral home. Ellen

28

in white ruffles? Ya, right. I guess that's how they dressed up bodies. It was not the real "her," at least. I used to adore the way the morning sun shone through her reddish brown hair. Her hair was still pretty in the coffin that night. But it was not the vibrant, so-alive Ellen who had graced my life for these five years. She would be smiling, grinning, laughing. This face was plastic, filled out with some kind of chemicals. I sat with her.

"Thank you for five wonderful years."

"Thank you for the muskrat walks, for putting up with Sunday afternoon football, and Wednesday night Criminal Minds, for chasing three a.m. meteor showers and autumn swan migrations."

"Thank you for those seven weeks of curiously bouncing through Western Europe, for exploring the country of Mauritius, for the late afternoon Moscow Mules and pinochle games."

"Sorry for not kissing you enough." I kissed her on her cheek. And I gave her a kiss from each of her siblings and her mom, as instructed.

Thou preparest a table before me in the presence of mine enemies: thou anointest my head with oil; my cup runneth over.

Death of spouse happens to others, not to me. That night, a loud party outside my hotel room spewed out awful, raucous music that only young people would appreciate. I retreated to hymns on my iPod. "Holy, holy, holy, Lord God Almighty." I will awake from this bad dream and it will all be okay. I whimpered. I stared and studied the ceiling. It will never be okay again. We were just riding the bikes. She told me she loved me. I looked over to the other bed to see if she was there. Where are you? At least, she was not in pain anymore: her feet, her heart, or any part of her.

Surely goodness and mercy shall follow me all the days of my life: and I will dwell in the house of the Lord forever.

Six cherubim appeared above me. They were pudgy, naked and small. I only recognized them, these fat little boys, because of my studies of Baroque art. They hovered above me for three or four seconds. Their figures were as clear as if they were right here, real, and present. Then they were gone.

And I will dwell in the house of the Lord forever...

Dr. Richard Brynteson is a professor, executive coach, innovation consultant, author, and public speaker. He teaches in the MBA program at Concordia University, St. Paul, where he has been a professor of 32 years. He has published six books, on business subjects such as innovation and behavioral economics. He has published blogs on his travels as well as thoughts on innovation and education. He has worked with companies on innovation projects in Africa, Asia, and the United States. He has only had to bribe his way out of jail once.

Straight and Narrow—X
Madaline

How can somebody you don't know look at you with such disdain in their eyes? They couldn't put themselves in your shoes, because they haven't been where you are. Some people may get it, but that's genuinely, because they have been through it. I'm not a people person, choosing solace in silence over mingling with judgmental strangers. Nobody's perfect, but Nobody's saint-like all the way around either.

Once upon a Savannah time, there had been magic in the air– swirling about, breathing hope into me. The hope would dissipate the more I would catch the eyes of some nasty person leering at me as if I'm the problem. People who aren't without a roof over their heads automatically assume it's a choice to live on the streets or in a tent. I have met one or two people who choose the life, but that's due to their drug habit or alcohol addiction. There are very few like my family and I, who are just trying to survive in order to escape this Hellish in between.

To clarify, it does not matter what you spend money on—the cost of living has skyrocketed which makes it harder for those of us trying to leave. You see; we don't all like to hang out with those in the same situation or go to the same places they go. Most of 'em are bad news, most especially when they get to drinking or shooting up. I hate needles; alcohol has never been a friend of mine. I've been led down the wrong path in my life more than likely to open a new door to something more.

Or so I'm hoping. At times, I don't understand why I'm still breathing. Is it because God hates me? Does he even really exist? Or are harder lessons on their way to teach me that life will never be what some chalk it up to be?

I want to have hope that if all these other people can make it then so can me, my brothers and sister. I won't know if we can make it until the opportunity presents itself. I'm beginning to think things were better as a kid due to how isolated I've become, but that's my own fault. I've seen people care just a little to have the spotlight on them. Do they really care about those of us, leading a hard life?

I do my best to obey the rules, follow the law, and keep on the straight and narrow path. It's difficult to do when less people believe in you. I'm a self-classified loner. I don't care for people— at the same time, I do (down deep, in my own twisted way). I'm not perfect, legitimately.

I was adopted. I've got scoliosis and bunions which are health problems that burden me. I can't say I think I love animals more than people, because I know I do. Animals will love you unconditionally whether you're homeless, disabled or mentally off your rocker. An animal won't judge you, because that's not how they are.

All of my life, I've dealt with watching cats be born; lending a hand to help raise them. It's nothing new for me. I've been homeless on and off with my siblings for a few years. Life never goes as we plan, expecting something different each time. I may have books published yet I don't generate an income from it.

Too many people don't have the money or they just dislike my books. I don't know– don't really care. I've got too much on my plate as it is. We ended up homeless due to shady people screwing us over; destroying our lives as they went along. I started in Florida, ended up in North Carolina, South Carolina, Georgia then North Carolina only to end up in Georgia once more.

We were trying to put down roots after we returned to Savannah, Georgia. We became homeless this last time due to a greasy, dirty, weasley roommate who conned my brother off his stimulus check. He conned those around him anyway, thinking people would like him for any length of time. He did nothing but make our lives miserable– messing up the apartment after it would be cleaned. He stank, hardly showering while claiming to be autistic.

How can you be autistic if you treat people so low and act like you're going to do them harm? Maybe, he was a different kind of autistic...? All I know is I did a background report on him; how many people have a long list of 'molesters' and still properly function? How many people try to fuck your family over after you leave Greenville, North Carolina to make a new start in the one place more like a home then the north? How many people try to steal your sister's disability check from afar?

His initials are RTL. He goes by his middle name. I tried to report him, but nothing. And yet, somebody still has the audacity to try to steal from my sister again from afar. There's no other cowards that I know– dumb enough to try this. So thanks to him, we left before he could boot us out.

We returned to Savannah, Georgia in late August of

2021. We were familiar with homeless camps before due to when we were first in Savannah. How long did we think it was going to last? Long enough to give us time to build up, but when you're trying to make a home out of a tent– you won't have much time to get out of this shithole. Ignorant people happen to think shelters are better than being on the streets let alone in a tent which is false.

We were in a shelter; Community Crossroads in Greenville, twice. Those in charge treat homeless people equally as bad, but home isn't about the people; it's about those in it. So, I guess the true homeless people are those with nothing to show for, but a roof over their heads. There is good, bad, and neutral in everything. I may not have a roof over my head yet I'm not going to claim myself as part of the "homeless community."

"Community" is another word for cult. Plain and simple. Other homeless people are just as bad if not worse than people in houses or apartments. There may be very few other homeless people who don't bother anyone else, opting to do their own thing. In fact, I've heard stories as such yet have never met one…I don't think Barry counts.

He seems to always have a crowd of troublesome, bothersome folk. Speaking of community and cults, churches are meant to be filled with God fearing people, yeah? God loves all of his children equally even those living a rough life. He wouldn't starve or judge those he brought into this world; giving us each a purpose. Sometimes, you'll find a snake– maybe, even a cult overflowing with snakes feigning as if their work is for God.

Not only is God the only one who can judge us, but you can't say you're Godly if you don't care enough to shoot someone a message asking about their wellbeing. Asking about somebody is a good show of friendship, compassion, and the way I'm sure God views it. Everybody's busy, even homeless people with nowhere to go. They think we don't try even when there's proof that says as much. How ignorant can this cult– this society of ours be? If you don't care then go about your merry way, but don't use God or religion to make yourself feel better and to seem like you're such a good person.

The cult leader of this church claims things that are hardly proven true. His followers and believers hang onto every word he says like the sheep that they are. You can be Godly, non-judgmental, and still be a decent human being especially those of us– you seemingly deem unworthy. I don't need religion to have God in my life; he's everywhere I go. Even though this cult had a partial hand in helping us, they never truly cared about us as human beings.

How do you know it's a cult? When every person present believes and thinks the exact same thing. Most of the time, you want somebody to challenge your views; not agree with the propaganda, bullshitting lies that you go around spewing. Think you're higher on the food chain? Then, why not try being without what some of us have to go without?

You won't think the same afterwards. At least, we would survive while y'all wimps would sink deeper than the ship you're on. We want change, but try living when you stay on the bottom consistently. I've been writing since I was a kid– crafting my own style. Has it worked?

I'm beginning to think I'm not good at what I do, but then again, what I write isn't for everybody. Most of it's more offensive, but I can't relate to censored things. I have trouble processing things especially where math is concerned. Lately, my trouble with processing has gotten worse. When people speak low or high; I still can't seem to grasp what they're saying.

I have conflict with yellers, having grown up in an abusive–dysfunctional household. My slow processing also makes it hard for me to speak right away, giving me a delayed reaction. I had a woman in Greenville call me retarded for overthinking, not being able to speak while having a panic attack. People don't understand the reality of anxiety even when they claim to have it. I say claim, because why treat somebody so low then?

Then again, I'm not perfect. So, who am I to say what somebody has? We all react differently even with anxiety. I should know better before casting the first stone. However, I won't tolerate somebody continuing to walk all over me either.

A bald headed man whose name I won't mention happens to steal, lie, cheat, and manipulate. This man is homeless. Do I know his situation? I don't care to know about somebody who can stab you every which way– metaphorically, speaking. I don't care to know about a man who wants to say your sister had a stroke and couldn't walk when the truth is; staph infection, or rather MRSA. He could have asked if he could have what we had to leave behind this last time rather than be a common thief with no morals for human decency.

He admitted a few things he tried to take to my sister. Talk about a loser. He's also a gossip queen trying to be in everybody's business, making fun of those who wouldn't do the same to him in turn. Of course, a person (let's say woman in this case), who publicly posts private messages is equally as bad especially when she's in the cult church group I mentioned prior.

Even if you got permission which she didn't, you still shouldn't go around being a sleaze ball of a human being– posting private conversations publicly for all of your non-existent friends to see. A friend to all is a friend to none; remember that, sis. Those messages were signed from me, not my sister on her Facebook. If you're gonna post something to start a war then do so, the right way. Of course, I'm no fighter unless I have to be.

Sis, we're putting things into motion. Stop harassing people like you're gonna know anything. As far as I'm concerned– hop on your bandwagon with your lame ass friends; ain't got time for fake ass bitches. You gave me an icky feeling; I knew I was right. Thank you for proving as much while we move on without y'all, as we get better.

I'm winding it down as quickly yet slowly as possible. Now, for the heated glares of stares from the Starbucks employees on Bay Street? Why are y'all so unhappy? Why try to make somebody feel uncomfortable in their own skin when some of us already do? You would have to be so unhappy with your own lives that it's not even funny.

Do y'all even know what freedom means? Then again, if y'all are locked into the ideology society has warped into everybody's brain– I guess, y'all wouldn't know what the word means. I'll be fine; with or without you. Karma is a very real thing– slow at times, but you'll surely reap what you sow. There's only one person I've ever talked to who genuinely cares about the wellbeing of those of us who were unlucky and unfortunate.

Someone she loves happens to be in the same boat, but has she forgotten about him? No, nor does she forget the rest of us either. Genuine concern is one thing– bullshitting people with careless action is another. Actions may speak louder than words yet that's not always true let alone sound advice. Also, humanitarians?

Let me ask you this; how can you be a humanitarian when you forget to care about people as people? Not for what they have or don't have. The world is lost, broken, isolated. We need to get back to real life versus fantasy land where life and creation go to die. Straight and narrow doesn't always exist, but in our case we're sticking to it– walking a straight line.

Very few people rarely care about people unless it benefits them. Someday, hopefully, soon, we'll get back to a not so careless world where the wellbeing of others are concerned. If this shit don't change then we'll all be dead. The only thing getting me through any of this is my love for music as well as the cats I've known since before their mother gave birth to them. I had another cat who mirrored my soul as well as traits personality wise– his name was Milkyway.

Savannah, Georgia is a beautiful place overflowing with mouthwatering food, people bustling about, and nice weather during the autumn-winter season. There's just some major downsides– the people aren't always what they're cracked up to be. The city itself is loaded to the top with crime and it's laced with darkness where secrets are concerned. I may have said it before, but some things are worth repeating. If you're a family unit, they'll try to break you up.

It's definitely not the same south I'm used to like the small town I grew up in. I just wish people had more heart and compassion for those around them. They don't seem to look outside the micro bubble they live in. SCAAD is full of pretentious, unwelcoming students whose 'daddy' bought their tuition– no doubt in my mind about it. I can't say all of SCAAD is bad though; there may be a small handful of students who don't mind sharing the same air every human on earth breathes.

They may also just be laughing at us behind our backs. Ain't there with them when they're off doing whatever so there's no good way of telling. It's usually in the body language and behavior of how people treat you. They'll ogle your animals, but treat you lower (and, I'm not even talking about SCAAD anymore). I liked Savannah briefly when we were first in the city, but my love has become bitter, distasteful hatred for this place.

It's not even just the place that makes me feel so at unease these days. It once felt like home. Due to the mistreatment of judgment brought on by the people of Savannah; this place most definitely doesn't feel like home anymore. I once felt like I belonged then everything changed; a shift in the air took place–putting us at odds with this place. Here's to hoping that the future becomes brighter.

Madaline is an author. Her first four novels are published through Ukiyoto Publishing House. She's a music lover, cat owner, Aries, Hufflepuff, triumphant loner. She lives somewhere in Georgia.

Requiem for a Contender
Clare Simons

When Dad was dying the nurses bound his hands in yards of Ace bandages so he couldn't pull out the life supports. The Buckeye Bomber, a Golden Gloves heavyweight champion, who fought the pro-circuit, Cleveland, Chicago Detroit, Kansas City, tough-guy towns—once on the same fight card as Joe Lewis—was down for the count. The boxers' hands were crossed, the right defending his face, the left, ready to punch.

But the final round was over.

I park my suitcase under a window and roll up the sleeves of my wool cardigan. The "Physicians Only" parking lot below Dad's room is filled with top-of-the-line luxury cars. Shining 1979 Lincolns, Caddys, Mercedes, and Jaguars reflect the day's last light of Fort Lauderdale's coast. I count the Cadillacs and watch Dad's nurse. Focusing on her helps me see the man I once feared. She finagles IV tubes and senses Dad's internal landscape. A blue hospital gown covers my father's body.

"Hello, Daddy," I say.

"We gave him something to help him rest. He knows you're here," the nurse says.

I inch my way across the room and kiss my Dad's bald head, charred from another round of radiation. A lone hair sticks to my lips. His body smells like a potion my grandmother concocted when our tomcat was dying. Graw mixed castor oil, iodine, and some fungus she scraped off a tree into a pulp, then plastered on the cat's wounds. Tom lived.

Dad opens his mouth as if to speak to me; mucus oozes out. I flee to the window and lean against the puke-green wall. The nurse swabs Dad's mouth with white gauze, cleans the sputum off the pillowcase, and discards the specimen in a red plastic receptacle marked Toxic. Death is messy. The nurse is going to heaven for such kindnesses.

I pray for my Father's swift death. May God forgive him his trespasses: drinking, gambling, flaunting his mistress, and hitting Mom. Forgive him for making me gasp for breath and cower when he set the draperies on fire.

God better forgive him because I cannot. Forgiveness from me isn't in the cards. I am numb and done. But then, another prayer flutters in my chest. It makes a foreign sound, like an exile from a cold land.

Mercy slips into my heart.

I bless the tender moments when High Roller Dad taught me to shoot craps, pick horses, and throw a punch. The nuns said these vices were unladylike, but Dad didn't care what those women said— they had repressed my dominant hand. I had forgotten my "natural inclinations." He is a southpaw and says I should be too.

"Don't take no bullshit," Dad says.

We work out in the basement below Dad's bar.

His gym is a speed bag on a stainless-steel swivel

mounted on the rafters, and a body bag he made from an Army canvas duffle stuffed with a roll of heavy carpet. He warms up by jumping rope, twisting and weaving it into precise patterns that make hissing and swooshing sounds as it cuts through the air. Dad jumps an inch; his leather shoes tap the concrete gently. My fifty-year old father can skip a three-minute round of double-unders and diagonals while I, a clumsy twelve-year old, trip on a front to back.

"Youse gotta stay in training," Dad says.

He brings down his brown leather Everlast boxing gloves from the shelf, and wraps my fingers and hands in Ace bandages, to protect them from being bent or smashed. He laces the gloves on me, so my wrists won't twist inside them. Dad's mitts make me feel powerful, ready to punch and jab, but I can't move. A boxer is his body; mine is too fat to spar. I weigh-in forty pounds more than the average sixth grader.

"The punch starts in the ball of your foot; spring off your heel, don't think about it," Dad says.

I hit the body-bag and miss. Hand-eye-foot coordination is too much to master, even though tiptoeing around Dad's periphery is my talent.

"Hit clean, the opponent is you," Dad says.

I could not float like a butterfly or sting like a bee, like his hero, Muhammad Ali.

Dad moves on to the black leather speed bag, "nev nev nev nev nev," it sings each time he hits it— faster than I can count— nev nev nev nev nev, a sound so subversive I want to cry, but that is not allowed so I pucker my lips and pout, nev nev nev nev nev, N-e-v-e-r will I make my father proud.

I raise my arms to box with God and graze the bag; "nev" it says.

"Let the bag come back to you. Stay light. Breath," Dad says.

I say the if only prayer. If only I had the power to force these hands and feet to punch there would be no jeers or boos or catcalls. If only I had the power to transform this body, be Dad's fit girl. If. Only.

Dad's life-lessons to a blossoming daughter are simple.

"Don't take no bullshit. Believe you can win. Fight clean."

Clare Simons' essays about Amma, India's hugging saint were published in *Parabola* and *Spirituality & Health* magazines. Her boxing essay *The Greatest* appeared on the official Muhammad Ali website along with works by Joyce Carol Oates and Norman Mailer. *Anti-Heroine Chic, bioStories, Faith Hope & Fiction, Manifest Station, Persimmon Tree* and *The Write Launch* published her creative nonfiction. Simons was the press person and gatekeeper to the stories of the terminally ill patient-plaintiffs defending Oregon's Death With Dignity Act at the U.S. Supreme Court, and worked for passage of assisted dying laws in several states. Publication of her memoir is forthcoming.

A Brief Remembrance of My Father

Jenn Zatopek

My father had moments of crystalline clarity in which he would say something that would stop me in my tracks, making me pause to catch my breath from the goodness found in his words. These brief times of peace with my father were sacred thresholds through which we would stumble together into stillness and rest awhile in the love that broke through. I recall them with great fondness because they were rare due to my father's troubles.

Dad's troubles began long before he attended UMASS in the fifties but the drinking didn't help. Imbibing more beer than other boys at parties, my father drank to forget the beatings my grandfather gifted him with. He kept drinking into his twenties and early thirties, kicking it with other reporters at the *Hartford Chronicle* for which he wrote investigative pieces taking him all over North America. After quitting reporting and moving to Maine, Dad tried Alcoholics Anonymous but found their reliance on a Higher Power distasteful and quit before he worked all the steps. Eventually my father found sobriety through aversion therapy and began working in childcare, where he learned to soothe his own little boy inside by caring for young children. The stint in childcare was brief, and after landing in Texas and a painful divorce in 1990, Dad became a single parent and machinist. He worked long nights with his turret lathe and unruly thoughts which churned inside him along with the hum of the machine shop.

I loved my father dearly, but I was terrified of his intense moods and incurring his wrath, which he often directed at me. He was estranged from himself, like a distant uncle who was beholden to wild rage and gripping sorrow. I couldn't discern what would set him off. His early years of abuse and eventual drinking in New England left him spent. In Maine, he basked in the glow of his newly found sobriety but he never quit that habit of rage in which he would lose control and punch walls or back me into a corner, his eyes alight with fire. After the tumult passed, he would become a child again, apologizing to me timidly and crying in regret. He never chose healing, but miraculously, small bursts of insight would break through. These moments with my father were bright lights against the dark and dismal skies of his untreated mood disorder and bitterness toward life.

We were standing in our living room filled with light, much like I'm seeing today, and I lamented about something, wondering if I'd be happier having been born in another time and place, wearing the heavy cloak of shame I'd been gifted with since childhood. *But Jennifer,* he said gently, using my childhood name with the bright sunshine hitting his face, *the best moment to live in is the one you're in now.* I stopped speaking for a moment before challenging him to explain what this meant. He said that the best time to be alive is right where your hands and your feet are, cherishing the moments you do have. Maybe some of this was wisdom gleaned from his short run in Alcoholics Anonymous. I like to believe Spirit helped to bring a bit of peace to a life filled with great suffering.

Even as I write this down I can't help but savor this beautiful moment, our living room at the apartment in North Texas in the mid-nineties, my old twin bed with the Southwestern comforter stuck against the wall behind us; the black-and-white television set on top of the milk crates on the shaggy brown carpet; the creamy oversized floor pillows near the opposite wall; my father's dark wooden New York desk, filled with old papers, silver coins, paperclips, drops of grease from his work as a machinist. We were one in that moment, both of us breathing easily for a little while, a rarity because I was in high school at the time, working long hours at the grocery store in high school while doing college classes to get a head start for university studies.

I don't remember what else happened after, whether I went off to my room to study or dressed for my shift at Albertsons or if he left to run errands or slam poetry in Dallas, a part of himself he refused to share with me. I don't remember if it was late afternoon when we stood and talked together. Was the evening sky tinged with blooming shades of indigo or was it the bright noonday sun we were seeing? Maybe the conversation veered completely off the path of peace because when you lived with someone who had mercurial moods and relied only on themselves for support, this sort of thing happened. There were sublime moments to be sure, moments of ecstatic joy and tender beauty, but they emerged inconsistently because of his unwillingness to seek treatment for his moods.

We desperately want our memories to connect to other joyful ones, leading to a life stringed with nothing but happiness, exiling the painful times into hiding. And yet as we open up to a deeper reality rooted in kindness, we can warmly embrace all our experiences, noting that our life with others is amazingly complex, inconsistent, rich, and even boring at times.

What I do remember is the radiance of my father's face as he turned toward the sun pouring through the glass patio doors, the brightness bathing us in a love which broke through the confines of a dark and lonely life. *Truly being here is so much; because everything here apparently needs us, this fleeting world, which in some strange way keeps calling to us. Us the most fleeting of all,* wrote the German poet Rainer Maria Rilke in *Duino Elegies*, and I know I touched the immensity of being as we stood in that radiance together.

As I reflect on this story now, I remember it not only as a sign of his love for me, *because he did love me,* and he was speaking to himself too, but as a sacred reminder of what's possible when I open my heart to the joy of the present moment, even as I recall the past. And when I return to that incandescent moment and give thanks for that brief moment of goodness, I come home to myself, smiling in recognition of being known and touched in love.

Jenn Zatopek is a writer and trauma-informed psychotherapist living in Texas. A native Texan with New England roots, Jenn writes at the intersection of science and faith, longing to encounter the divine in the most unexpected places. Her work has been featured in *Ruminate Magazine, Fathom,* and elsewhere. More at Jenn's website theholyabsurd.com, or follow her on Instagram @theholyabsurd.

Nursing Mother
Rachel Lutwick-Deaner

"A mother who has had a baby in the hospital should insist on keeping him with her 24 hours a day. Unwrap the baby, keep him in your bed, and don't allow a pacifier to be given. Watch for your baby's subtle signals that he's ready to nurse again—trying to suck on his hands or the blanket, turning his head from side to side as though searching for the breast, making smacking or sucking noises, or whatever cues your individual baby uses to signal you. Responding to these messages and feeding the baby will help prevent engorgement and encourage the development of a good milk supply"[1]

A child who has had a mother in the hospital will insist on keeping the mother with her 24 hours a day. Wrap up the mother, keep her by your bed, and don't allow your father to annoy her. Watch for your mother's subtle signs that she is in pain—furrowing her brow, sighing loudly, making a hissing sound, white knuckles, or whatever cues your individual mother uses to signal you. Responding to these messages and helping the mother will help prevent discord and encourage the healing process.

When a person you love is sick, you want to find a way to make them better. When you have already spent time inside that person, you want to crawl back inside once more to take the pain, poison, rot away. That's what I was doing in the days following my mother's mastectomy, when I stripped the drains of her incision, carefully peeling tape, replacing bandages, drawing the blood and seroma fluid away from her body, milking her wounds with more precision and focus than her babies ever drew milk from her now absent breast.

"Milking the drain may seem like an odd expression, but 'milking the drain' keeps the tube from getting clogged...WIth one hand, hold the tube where it enters your body. Keep this hand in place so you do not tug on your skin...With your fingers pinched, slide your fingers down the tube...Milk the drain every three hours during the day while you are awake. You do not have to wake up and do this at night."[2]

The connection between stripping the drain and breastfeeding cannot be ignored. Mothers pour their bodies into their newborns unselfishly, it seems, but there is an invisible tubing that leads from that tiny body to the adult hands that will one day strip that drain, pulling the clots, tissues, blood, seroma fluid away from mother's body.

Before my first baby, Tali, was born, I acquired a book loftily titled *The Ultimate Breastfeeding Book of Answers: The Most Comprehensive Problem-Solving Guide to Breastfeeding from the Foremost Expert in North America.* This book is authored by Dr Jack Newman and Teresa Pitman, and together they take a no-nonsense, listen-up-you-silly-ninny tone with the new mother. This tone seemed to work for me, as leading up to the birth of my first child I was confident that *of course* I would nurse her, it would work out fine, and I knew exactly what to do. I had read enough of the book to get to the passage "Put Part A into Part B" (perhaps oversimplifying the steps in my reading). I looked at the pictures of the various holds.

Cradle hold: Baby's round tummy atop your own jiggly middle, sweet button nose right at the nipple for a good latch, baby's head cradled in the crook of your arm.

Cross cradle hold: Similar to the cradle, but this time the arm opposite your breast cradles baby.

Football hold: Now baby is tucked under your arm, allowing your horrific GERD to stay silent for a few moments.

It all made sense.

I knew what to do. No problem. This is what mothers do to take care of their babies.

In anticipation of your mother's surgery, you'll want to watch a YouTube video of how to strip the drains. You won't want to, but you will. There are many–you may want more than one just to feel like you've had the full experience before you stand in front of your mother. She will be frail after 14 weeks of chemotherapy. She will be rumpled, from a night of discomfort. She will smell like toothpaste and unwashed hair and hospital disinfectant. You will smile. You will tell her to sit down on the toilet seat while you take care of this. You will begin. "This will be no problem," you tell her. "This is what daughters do for their mothers," you think. It pales in comparison to the millions of things she has done for me over the years. I remember her carefully selecting the right paper cups and plastic table cloth for my 5 year old birthday party–how she poured the vivid red drinks for the children, the red liquid a shocking strawberry color, matching the lurid red cap that Strawberry Shortcake wore on my bakery cake.

You will look at your mother, her careful hands, small fingers, artfully manicured, the same hands that smoothed your wedding gown, that held your arm to steady you after a fall, that cradled your infant head.

You will wash your hands as if you are praying. *Al netilat yadim* prayers aside, you are about to do something holy. Every video instruction you watched prompted you to wash your hands well, faucet at full throttle, soap breathing life into suds. You will wash away your skin as the surgeon did, flesh becoming absence.

"We always hold the tubing close to the body to prevent unnecessary tugging that can be painful to the patient"[3]

You will need to have confidence as you grip the first drain, as close to the incision as you can get. Do not be squeamish. Do not be overconfident. You might hurt her more than she has already been hurt. Pinch the drain at the top with one hand, and use your thumb and forefinger to drag the fluid, mostly blood and seroma, down the length of the tubing. It will be surprisingly warm. The blood will reluctantly part from the tubing. It will smell like sickness but not death. You will coax and pull that fluid out of your mother's wound, and you will collect it in a plastic bulb.

You will relish the stripping of the drains, because it's measurable. You keep track of the milliliters of fluid in a little journal, like you tracked the diaper changes of infancy. Much of cancer is measurable—stage of the tumor, weeks of chemo and radiation, length of incision, number of stitches—but you can measure this yourself. Everything else has been done to your mother, but this you can do for her.

You could do nothing for her tumor. A rosette that pulsed and glistened and bled.

"Mom," I joked over the phone when she was first diagnosed, "How about I just do an at home extraction with nail scissors?"

Frustrated that the process of cancer treatment seemed to drag on, I (only half joking) suggested she just go and sit at the hospital until they agreed to cut it out. Normally the biggest fan of my outrageous declarations, my mom did not indulge my humor. She would follow the oncologist and the surgeon's recommendations. Certainly, I thought in my desperation, there was a way to strangle the tumor, to let it wilt and die before my mother had to. Die.

You tried to help out by sending books, cards, a mastectomy camisole with special hook ups for the tubing, hats to keep her naked head warm, v-neck t-shirts for easy access to the port, robes so fuzzy they clogged the dryer vent. You've made chicken soup five different ways, for healing; brewed batches of lemon ginger tonic, for soothing; assembled custard slice, for nostalgia. But nothing feels as good as stripping the drains.

"You are going to open that little stopper in the drain. Make sure to open it away from you because you don't want it to splash you in the face"[4]

You will pour the fluid into the measuring cup, hands shaking almost imperceptibly. You will write down the ccs of fluid in a log. Completing the drain log feels industrious. You will write the numbers crisply, entering dates, times, amounts.

December 13, 2020. 8:15 am. L: 8ml R: 5ml
December 13, 2020. 9:45 pm. L: 7ml R: 6ml
December 14, 2020. 7:46 am. L: 10ml R: 6 ml

My handwriting is shaky, and my mom notices when I've written the information in the wrong column, chiding my careless work. I am reminded of the earnest way I kept track of those early nursing sessions.

April 4, 2003. 7:05 am. L: 35 min R: 25 min

April 6, 2003. 11:45 am. L: 60 min (fell asleep) R: 20 min

April 7: 2003. 1:00 pm. L: 25 min R: 15 min

The fluid will look like the Kool Aid from your five year old birthday party. Almost delicious but also terrible. The videos even use the word Dixie Cup to describe where you should pour it to measure. While your mother poured so many cups of Kool Aid to the already over-stimulated and over-sugared party guests, you fill only two cups with red.

"This fluid can then go down your toilet" [5]

You will empty the measuring cup in the toilet, and it will look like so many bowls full of menstrual blood, postpartum blood. Blood that blooms and shimmers in the clear waters of the toilet. Vibrant, living, the inside turned out.

You will help your mother replace the drain bulbs, zip up the compression garment, carefully snake her arms back into a button up shirt. She is tucked away before you wash out the cup in the kitchen sink, because where else will you do it? You will think about your mother's cells, her body going down the drain, and you will think about the other parts of her that are now gone, in a dumpster or incinerator somewhere, and how much of her has been dispersed already. How many ounces her four babies sucked away, how many ounces of her breast, her tumor, disposed of.

In order to encourage milk production, new mothers should keep their calorie intake up. *"In northern Europe, brewer's yeast and beer were thought to increase milk supply. In southern China, fish and papaya soup. In various places, different herbs, probably depending on what was available locally. Borage, alfalfa, fenugreek, raspberry leaf, fennel, blessed thistle, goat's rue–these are just some of the various herbs that have been thought to increase milk supply"*[6]

I remember going to A Southern Season, a mecca of delicacies, and buying Izze sodas. I needed sweetened beverages–I needed to tantalize myself to keep up the milk supply.

I ordered the chicken salad on croissant the first time my mother-in-law and I took baby Tali out to a cafe, even though my mother-in-law would never order that lunch for herself–too fattening. I could tell she was pleased for me to eat it though. She looked forward to seeing the baby's cheek round out, the rolls on the little thighs.

I got the premium ice cream—Ben and Jerry's Chubby Hubby or New York Super Fudge Chunk. If I only had a few minutes to spoon it up before my baby cried for me, I had to make it count.

I got Morning Glory muffins from Whole Foods, Chocolate oreo cake from the Mad Hatter, full fat Brown Cow yogurts from Harris Teeter, things I could eat standing and with one hand, because if you don't nutrify, you may not have the energy to take care of the baby the way you need to.

In order to fight the cancer, patients should keep their calorie intake up.

The scene of my mother's cancer diagnosis and treatment was Eau Claire, WI. Eau Claire is at once the same drab big box stores along depressing highways as every town in America and a unique and beautiful mix of old industrial town and modern art and music hub, all at the confluence of the Eau Claire and Chippewa rivers, two mighty streams of water like tubes connecting to form one channel, pulling towards an outlet.

There's not a lot to do in Eau Claire, especially during the Covid epidemic. When I arrived in town to be a support person during the early weeks of my mother's treatment, I learned quickly that there are only two things I could do consistently in Eau Claire, WI: walk, across bridges and trails following the rivers, and eat.

When I say eat, I mean eat treats, because there is no shortage of delicious baked goods in the upper Midwest.

Among the delights that I bought for my mother to encourage her calorie intake include:

Kolachkes-those filled Czech rolls that could be sweet or savory. How my father loved the sausage and cheese. I ate them too.

Raspberry swirl coffee cake, also chocolate chip coffee cake and rhubarb coffee cake.

Olsen's ice cream: Chocolate monster, brownie batter, Raspberry truffle, butterscotch swirl, butter pecan.

Pies! Lingonberry, strawberry rhubarb, pecan, fudge pecan, death by chocolate, chocolate peanut butter, raspberry sour cream. From the Norske Nook, only.

My mother didn't want most of the goodies that my father and I purchased. Dad and I would leave them on the counter, offer to cut a slice and put it on a plate–bring it to her on the couch, in a chair. She might accept the offer, but she would leave it to grow stale and brittle. Dad would ask again, "Can I get you anything?" and she would decline. Not interested. Dad would look stricken, and then I would cut a hunk for myself. I needed all the calories I could get to be the caregiver, just as I had upped the calories I needed to keep my milk up for those all night nursing sessions.

"The first question we should be asking is, Why are we concerned about weight gain? More particularly, why is it necessary for babies to gain a certain amount of weight each day or each week or each month?"[7]

Successful feeding is a way to quantify wellness. Every checkup is a victory for a nursing mother, every weigh in, when you gingerly place your baby atop the infant scale, carefully removing her diaper so as not to confuse the scale, each added ounce is a sign that you are doing your job, feeding that baby. My babies were gloriously fat with neck rolls and bracelets of chub around their wrists. Their cheeks ballooned, weighing their heads down, and they were perfect, so perfectly healthy.

"Proper positioning and latching on are crucial to success. For most mothers and babies, this is the most important step. "Latching on" refers to the way the baby takes the breast into his mouth. A good latch means pain-free breastfeeding; it also means that the baby will get the milk he needs and you will be on your way to a successful breastfeeding experience"[8]

I have no memories of myself as a nursing babe, but I do recall nursing my own three babies.

My babies were quick to master the latch, and before the lactation consultant could even suggest the football hold, they were putting on the ounces, surpassing birth weight, before we even left the hospital. I watched their cheeks work and heard the whoosh of milk, their happy grunts fading as they fell into milk drunk slumbers. I let them sleep on the breast, because why not. It felt good to nurture them, to give them what they needed. The milk bar was open all night long, and we took to sleeping side by side, me dozing on and off as baby kept a full tank all night long.

"How tiring is it, really, for a mother to lie in bed with her baby beside her, sucking at her breast?. . . As long as mother and baby are together, there is no rush"[9]

In the first foggy weeks of my babies' lives, I spent hours, days, eyes locked on their tiny wrinkled faces, hands like miniature starfish, nails tiny translucent daggers, impossibly hairy foreheads, breathing them in, memorizing their tiny bodies, mesmerized by their heady scent, nursing, and nursing, and nursing. They all had their different habits: Tali reached out to "protect her treasure"--guarding the idle breast until she was done feeding on the first; Zev would get so excited to nurse, he would tense his legs so they stood out straight, rigid; Davita scratched rhythmically as she nursed with gusto--you could hear the milk gushing into her mouth from across the room.

"Once the baby is sucking but not drinking, just nibbling, the mother should start with the breast compression. The baby should be sucking, but not actually drinking (open mouth wide–pause–close type of sucking). As the baby sucks, the mother, who is holding her breast with one hand, the thumb on one side and her other fingers on the other side of the breast, with a good amount of the breast in her hand, should just bring her thumb and fingers together, compressing the breast. This should be done firmly, but not so hard that it hurts"[10]

In 2003, as I waltzed my fussy baby Tali around our tiny bungalow in Durham, North Carolina, my husband asked, *Is any baby held and cuddled as much as our baby?* Without much consideration, I replied, *I just don't want her to be a serial killer one day.*

Is it as simple as that? I don't want her to be a serial killer. I don't want her to self-harm. I don't want her to be cold, withholding, cruel. 20 years later, in a space where my babies approach adulthood as my parents approach infirmity, I'm acutely aware that the baby I once nursed all night long may one day milk my body once more, stripping the drains.

For some people, nursing is painful and short lived. I nursed all of my babies for over a year because it was easy. It felt like that's what I was supposed to be doing. I both wanted to and had to do it. For the baby, and for myself.

Taking care of my mother in her illness felt the same. It was easy to take care of her. I both wanted to and had to do it. For my mother, and for myself.

As a newborn, our physical self is determined by the other, the mother. As a mother, in many ways our physical self is determined by the nursing babe. As a cancer patient, recovering from surgery, our physical self is determined by the surgeon, the physical therapist, the caregiver. As the adult child, caring for the mother, our physical, emotional, our psychic, self is determined by the other–the mother–and our proximity to her.

"I don't want you to leave," my mother says, as I gather my things.

Don't leave me

I know she doesn't really mean it, that she knows the rest of the family has been missing me at home.

Don't leave me

I've been here at her side with those words on my lips all week. Those words on my lips for the past six months. Those words on my lips, falling out of my throat, for the last forty-five years.

Don't leave me

1 - Newman, J., and T. Pitman. *The Ultimate Breastfeeding Book of Answers.* Three Rivers, 2006, p. 102.

2 - "Going Home after Breast Cancer Surgery with Drains." *YouTube*, YouTube, 19 Mar. 2021, https://www.youtube.com/watch?v=PnZP94A8psA.

3- "How to Properly Care for Your Surgical Drain - Moffitt Cancer Center." *YouTube*, YouTube, 12 June 2017, https://www.youtube.com/watch?v=OUzMN63faf4.

4 - "How to Empty a JP Drain | Edina Plastic Surgery." *YouTube*, YouTube, 7 Feb. 2022, https://www.youtube.com/watch?v=JvpAieP1C-k.

5 - "How to Empty a JP Drain | Edina Plastic Surgery." *YouTube*, YouTube, 7 Feb. 2022, https://www.youtube.com/watch?v=JvpAieP1C-k.

6 - Newman, J., and T. Pitman. *The Ultimate Breastfeeding Book of Answers.* Three Rivers, 2006, p. 73.

7 - Newman, J., and T. Pitman. *The Ultimate Breastfeeding Book of Answers.* Three Rivers, 2006, p. 64.

8 - Newman, J., and T. Pitman. *The Ultimate Breastfeeding Book of Answers.* Three Rivers, 2006, p. 50.

9 - Newman, J., and T. Pitman. *The Ultimate Breastfeeding Book of Answers.* Three Rivers, 2006, p. 45.

10 - Newman, J., and T. Pitman. *The Ultimate Breastfeeding Book of Answers.* Three Rivers, 2006, p. 72.

Rachel Lutwick-Deaner enjoys a bookish life. She earned a BA in English from Colgate University, an MA in English Literature from North Carolina State University, and a MFA from Queens University of Charlotte. She currently resides in Grand Rapids, MI, where she teaches college composition and literature at Grand Rapids Community College. Rachel delights in writing essays that challenge and affirm her readers, and her ultimate goal is to make people laugh, even uncomfortably. When she's not writing or teaching, Rachel loves reading, and her book reviews can be found at *Southern Review of Books* and on Instagram @professor.ld.

End to the Year Long Winter
John Ganshaw

It's been over a year of darkness, and I am longing for the light of a new dawn. The memories of what brought me to this place are so surreal. It seems like it should have been a dream, but all is still there every morning when I awake. This reality is so difficult for me and those around me. They hate you for what you did and are doing, yet, for some reason I can't. Is it because of how much I love you still, or is it because I believed in you, who you were, and who you could be? I am sure that after many therapy sessions, it will be decided that it was a combination of both. I still can't believe you did this to me, the person you said you would never hurt. You have cut me a thousand times by what you have done. The scars will always be visible to me, running long and deep. I want to believe that they will heal and be less visible in time. I have so many doubts, I see all that you did every time I look in the mirror, a skeleton covered in flesh, hardly resembling the man I once was. The only thing you didn't damage was the compassion and love that resides within me, still able to be seen through my eyes. Should I thank you for at least leaving me this, probably not.

The lies, the untruths you told the police, not to mention the money you paid, to have me arrested. All you did, caused me to spend the last year in a Cambodian prison, fighting for my innocence. Even now, I defend you because I know you didn't do this on your own. You may have pulled the trigger, but your puppet master created you and pulled the strings. You were just a toy that could be manipulated for his enjoyment, once I was out of the way, he left you to fend for yourself, once I was released on bail just a few months ago, he left the country. A prison is an interesting place and while there I learned so much about you, and what he did to you and your brother. The atmosphere you put me in allowed me to arrange all the pieces of your puzzle and see the complete picture of you for the first time. Now, the tears are still being shed but not so much for you anymore, for the people I came to know and who became an extended family. I can never forget what you did. The man I came to know and loved had a beautiful caring heart. I could see it when I looked into your eyes. I wish you would have confided in me and told me about the life he created for you: the misdeeds you were doing and the illness he gave you, physically and mentally. I still feel your tears as they strike my shoulders, hearing you repeating, "I'm sorry, I should have told you the truth." The person you refer to as your master raped you and your brother, pimped you out, and he made you extort money from your tricks through making videos. Forced you to blackmail others. Your actions provided me with the opportunity to see the world through the eyes of others. To see what the real world was like for many people living in a third-world country. Other men have been incarcerated for false charges and being unable to pay the authorities. At the age of 58, I am realizing the truth to the saying, "Everything has its price." You thought being in prison would kill me, that I would die, and with my death the truth of what happened, and the truth about your owner and what he was doing. I am very much alive and stronger than before.

The men of block D, cell #9 were just twenty-three of such people who taught me so much about the Cambodian judicial system. Hearing their stories and predicaments motivated me to fight for them once I was free and back on safe soil. Each one of them is unique and all of them, together, took care of me. We in the West are so fortunate that we don't always take the time to appreciate all that we have, not just the material. The stories of Baut, Boy, Chantha, and Vin are just four raindrops in the lake of injustice.

Baut was only 23 years old and arrested for using ICE, the drug of choice here in this Kingdom of Wonder. So many stories about this miracle drug, each one similar, and the power it has can make you forget about all your troubles. The drive provides you endurance and strength to perform, sexually and while on the job. Baut told me that when you have no hope ICE makes all your problems disappear. You forget that you don't have a job and that it is almost impossible to earn a decent living. You don't care that you have no money to buy food for the family. You forget all your troubles. He didn't receive many visitors and no packages because his family lived so far away from the prison. Yet, he still smiles every day. He accepted that this was his lot in life, and he couldn't change it. He was sentenced to fifteen months. As I write this, he should be free to be with his wife and child again. The sad realization is that with drug use, most end up back in prison.

Boy was 35 and his crime, he cut down a tree that wasn't his. He was sentenced to five years but reduced to twelve months. Boy's family fled Cambodia during the civil war in the '80s, though Khmer, was born in Thailand. He can't read the

Khmer language, only the spoken word. He attended a Thai school but dropped out after the sixth grade to work and help his parents. Boy was the cooker for our cell and a very good one at that. Each morning he would rise early, gather any wasted plastic bottles we had in the cell, to build a fire for boiling water. He did this to ensure that another older man and I would be able to have a cup of coffee. Once the coffee was ready, I would feel him gently pulling on my foot, a wake-up call for me to join them. He would then gather the ingredients from the various eating groups and proceed to prepare them for cooking. Measure out the rice provided by our families and friends. Takedown the preserved salted meats and fish that were hung the day before. In addition to these daily duties, he watched over our most valuable provisions, ensuring cookies, noodles, cocoa, and candies that had been brought to me were secured. No one, in my whole time there, ever stole from me. Evidence of mutual respect was always on display.

Kevin was a cellmate of mine from almost the very beginning. He arrived a day after me and was freed two weeks before I was granted bail. His crime, someone posted a Voice of America video to his YouTube channel. For this, he spent six months in prison and lost his job with an NGO. He would eventually become our cell team leader, we weren't referred to as prisoners or inmates, but rather we were referred to as members. This was not a club med or timeshare by any stretch of the imagination. Unless of course, your idea of a holiday is sleeping on the floor with 23 others, in a space the size of maybe 18 x 9. If so, your amenities include a squat toilet, (make sure you put a flip-flop in the hole at night to prevent unsavory critters from coming to visit), and a trash can to fill with water for your bucket showers. PS, make sure you put a cloth over the hose to catch the little pieces of metal; once inside your body they can cause a lot of discomfort and do considerable damage. There is no extra charge for the bacteria and the multitude of infections that can fall upon you. As a bonus, each guest gets a complimentary case of scabies, with a side of staph infections.

Back to Vin, he was a great leader. He ensured everyone was provided for, and that all food groups were equally divided so no member had to just eat the provided fish head soup and lowest quality rice. Vin was a college-educated, artist, writer, and all-around good guy. While we were speaking one day it was discovered that his best friend was also a friend of mine. Strange things happen, I guess. We would spend endless amounts of time discussing the importance of education and the political climate throughout the world. So much misery is overlooked by foreign governments, all in the name of the almighty profit and what is in it for them. He would often say how he dreamed that after all this was over for us, including Chantha, to be able to work together for sustainable change. He was and is so wise, well beyond his years. Now that we are both out, we chat just about every day. The difference is that he was free, I was just out on bail, waiting for justice to be served. Each day I began to realize that this was Cambodia, so the chance of justice was slim to none. The darkest of circumstances can carry some bright light, and that was the people I met and if it wasn't for the lies and false charges, I never would have met them.

Chantha, oh my god, Chantha. He too was by me since the day I arrived, taking care of me from the first moment we met. He would bring me candy, noodles, and iced coffee and this was before we were in the same cell. From the instant our eyes locked, I knew he had a beautiful soul and was a caring person. During the time we were in prison, Chantha's wife gave birth to their third child. Each morning he would look at a photograph of his family, say a prayer, and smile. This was his motivation to fight. He owned a farm and worked for an NGO until false charges were filed against him. Like me, those who want something you have can go a long way to get what they desire. In his case, a father and son who also worked for the NGO wanted his job, no problem. The son's wife filed charges that Chantha raped her. Now he was facing a similar fate to mine. Though we were completely innocent we had to fight the charges on appeal. Chantha was the first person to explain the full process and how it all comes down to arranging a package, (money,) for the court. Chantha was given a job in our block, to keep a record of the health of all the members. He would relay information to the infirmary and try to secure medicines. It was almost impossible to get medicines from the infirmary, the correction officers sold the medicines on the black market. To get medicines that were needed, Chantha would get word to his wife, and she would deliver them in a care package. To be given this job he had to pay a sum of a hundred dollars to the correction officer in charge. To supplement the medicines needed, Vin and I would also rely on medicines and bandages supplied by our friends who brought care packages. Soon, others within the block knew that if they had an ailment they would come to see us for bandages, medicines, etc.

From what Chantha told me of his parents and siblings, though all seem to be truly amazing individuals, he is most like his father. Chantha told me his father was a teacher yet he managed to survive the genocide of the Khmer Rouge. He did this because he was able to build ox carts, ox carts that the Khmer Rouge desperately needed. Having that ability not only allowed him to survive the killing fields but enabled him to employ ten other teachers, thereby saving their lives as well. Chantha inherited his father's mechanical skills, he was the person who taught me how to make an oil burner out of a sardine can twine out of an empty bread bag, and a water filtration system. Our dates of appeal were only two days apart so maybe, with some hope, we can all be together again, on the outside, and begin discussing how to facilitate change to a broken system. To plot how we can seek change and hope for those less fortunate than us.

These four individuals and so many others changed my life forever. They taught me about overcoming adversity. The need to fight when you don't want to fight anymore. That compassion exists everywhere if you are willing to look. That even in the darkness there is light. They made me a better person.

Once out on bail, I wasn't free and still felt incarcerated. I was actually under house arrest. Afraid to go anywhere, that I would be rearrested and put back in prison. The guilt I felt for being on the outside was unbearable. I would start crying and shaking while riding in the tuk-tuk. I would go grocery shopping and find myself crying while standing in front of the Coke display. Fear had taken hold; constantly thought I saw the people responsible for trying to kill me. I was told it was normal for someone with PTSD to come to terms with what happened.

Today I sat on the terrace of my friend's house, friends who had taken me in until I was free and able to leave for the USA, it would no longer be safe for me to live in Cambodia, the place I called home. The sun was shining and the sky an eye-piercing blue. Birds chirping, roosters crowing, butterflies meandering and fluttering through the air. It was all a reminder that I survived and was breathing. People kept telling me to be thankful that I was still alive, but was I? The heat and warmth of the sun still left me freezing like ice inside. I knew that I would never be the same person I was, that man had met his peril. Though they didn't physically kill me, they succeeded in killing the person I was. On that day I noticed a sprout breaking its way through the surface, a new beginning waiting to burst out, a new life being born. The clouds appeared to be drifting away, a fresh and glowing dawn would soon be on the horizon, for all of us.

John Ganshaw: After 31 years in banking, John (he/him) retired to follow his dream of owning a hotel in Southeast Asia. This led to many new experiences enabling John to see the world through a different lens, leading him to write his story through essays, poetry, and a yet unpublished memoir. John's work has appeared in *Native Skin, Rats Ass Review, eMerge, Post Roe Alternatives, Fleas on the Dog, OMQ, Disabled Tales, Unlikely Stories,* and many others. Nothing is as it seems in life, and experiences are meant to shape us not define us. Live for hope, truth, and adventure, which provide the stories that need to be written and told.

Escaping A Predator

Sharon Oberne

I was club hopping with my BFF, Jeannie, when I found myself in deep trouble! This was the 1970's and it was quite popular to go to a discotheque to meet someone to date. These dancing clubs were springing up across the Tampa Bay area and we were always interested in checking out the newest one.

So, we ended up at a discotheque on Dale Mabry Highway. Upon entering the building, I noticed a large python displayed in a glass enclosure. The word "predator" struck me like a ton of bricks, but "prey" never entered my mind. Seeing the snake should've been a warning, because that evening I would become the prey for another predator.

Jeannie and I ordered the "ladies' night special" the club offered, which was a large paper cup filled with ice and wine. The cost was only one dollar. We managed to find an empty table, sit, and slowly sipped on our drinks. It didn't take long for the club to become packed with young men and I was asked to dance.

His real name was William, but he liked being called, "Billy." Billy was rather tall and not much of a dancer. When he asked about getting some fresh air, I didn't hesitate, since the place was overcrowded.

Once we made it outside, there were a few people hanging around. I didn't know Billy was a predator at that time, since I didn't get a weird feeling being around him. Later, I would learn Billy assumed there wasn't anyone in the parking lot, so he could force me into his car and take off. Therefore, he had to come up with an alternate plan.

Billy convinced me he was an undercover narc and had some weed in his car that he needed to get. I asked him what he was doing with a joint, if he were an undercover agent. He came up with a good story about getting arrested for carrying weed and instead of having to serve time behind bars, he was released as long as he became a snitch.

Billy needed to get a joint from his car and sell it to a potential customer, someone in the parking lot, to meet his weekly quota for helping the police. I asked him why he would do such a thing, and he claimed if the person was dumb enough to buy it, then that person deserved some time in jail.

I walked over to his car and stood near the door, watching as he fumbled around, looking for this so-called joint. Since he couldn't find the non-existent joint, he picked up a pack of cigarettes off the dashboard, removed one and lit it up. He asked if I'd wait for him to finish and then we'd go back inside.

Billy reached over and unlocked the passenger door and insisted I should sit while he finished his cigarette. Once I sat down, with the car door opened, he started up the car. He completely caught me off-guard, as he drove away. He mumbled about going to his place to get a joint.

I thought about jumping out of the moving car, but for

some reason I can't explain, I felt it was better if I didn't.

We weren't far from the club, when he pulled into a driveway. Since it was dark, I could barely make out a small wooden house. Billy ordered me to stay seated and not to get out of the car, and after he said that, my stomach began to act up. I had a strong feeling he was testing me. I just knew if I'd left the car, I'd become his prey.

Once Billy returned, he took me back to the club. There was no more mention about selling a joint. I told him that Jeannie was probably worried about me and I needed to head back inside. Billy went with me and followed me as I walked over to where Jeannie was sitting with some guy. We made eye contact, and I mentioned about heading home, since it was getting late, and we had church tomorrow.

I said goodbye to Billy, but he blocked me from leaving. Literally, he stood in my way and commanded, "You will be back here next week, is that understood?"

"Of course," I lied, staring up at him. As he walked away, I knew he was convinced I'd keep my promise.

Jeannie and I didn't say a word until we were in my car and out of the parking lot.

"What was that all about?" asked Jeannie.

"I don't know! Something is wrong with that guy!"

"I can't believe you went outside with him!"

"Neither, can I!"

Wearing a grin on her face, Jeannie couldn't help herself and asked, "Are you coming back next week?"

"HELL, NO!"

I don't know how long it was before I read the headlines about a serial killer named William Mansfield, Jr., otherwise known as Billy, who buried his victims on his parents' property in Hernando County. At first it didn't click, until I saw his picture and his car. Yes, indeed, I was just plain lucky not to become one of Billy's victims.

Sharon Oberne (pen name: Sharon Brown) has always felt like a magnet, since she seems to attract predators. As such, she is the author of *Innocence Splattered*, which is available on Hoopla, *Born Magnet: Innocence Splattered* Ebook by Sharon Brown | hoopla (hoopladigital.com) and other digital platforms.

Somewhere Else

Keith A. Barker

Tension: On the Way to Robben Island by Keith A. Barker. 2013. Digital print.

The Catholic sister smiled kindly as she pushed the button for the gate to close, leaving me alone on the curb. Before dawn in Johannesburg, South Africa, I stood outside the Catholic compound where the rest of the members in my traveling group still slept. The hazy fatigue of jetlag made my bones feel like lead. Back home I would have been heading to bed about now, but here the day had barely begun. Back home, summer was in full swing, but here the cool breeze whispered late fall. For this, my first trip to South Africa, I'd made special arrangements for a side-trip on one of our first mornings there before our group's itinerary began. Though my objective for that day was Sterkfontein Cemetery, I had no idea where I was going, was in search of someone's grave whom I'd never met, and anything resembling success required dependence on others. A small red Audi pulled up and pulled me out of my thoughts and on to my journey.

My time in South Africa had all the makings of any great trip abroad: the beautiful, gratifying vistas, the new appreciation for the familiar and the unfamiliar, the *carpe diem* motivation each morning, and—no matter what you think about the indelible British influence and how it got there—the afternoon tea is wonderful. Beyond all that, this fascinating country gave me a renewed sense of the world's geographical and historical immensity, and my small part of the whole.

I had been reading G.K. Chesterton's engaging *Father Brown* series of short fiction, which features a beloved parson who solves baffling mysteries armed with wit, and world-wise perspectives gained in part from his parishioners' confessions. Amid the unfolding of one such mystery, Father Brown is asked as clergy, if he thought there is any ultimate meaning in the world, and if we all really will have to answer to a final, inevitable end; the kind of retribution and reconciling in which all that has happened will be sorted out and judged. He answered in the affirmative: "We here are on the wrong side of the tapestry. The things that happen here do not seem to mean anything; they mean something somewhere else. Somewhere else retribution will come on the real offender. Here it often seems to fall on the wrong person."

While South Africa is not that heavenly "somewhere else" land of clarified meaning, reconciliation, and ultimate truth for which our hearts yearn, it merely points as a sign to that perfection. In the meantime, the wrong people get the short end of the stick.

What I had known about Africa was through vicarious experience. Family members and friends had lived and worked on the continent for decades. For example, Lilburn Adkins, and his wife, Florence, were missionaries there for many years. Lilburn grew up an orphan in western Kentucky and went on to attend Asbury College where he fell in love and later married Florence Northcott. After graduating in 1922, he took his bride to work as missionaries in Africa. By the late 1950s they had lived almost three decades in East Africa, and then finally moved to Krugersdorp, near Johannesburg, to live among the Africans working in and around the gold and diamond mining operations there.

On the evening of February 12, 1961, Lilburn and Florence walked home from an evening church service, having taken the train. Their car was in the shop in anticipation of their daughter visiting with their new son-in-law later that month. After disembarking the train, they realized there were no taxis at the station, and so they were forced to make the 25-minute walk home in the dark.

On the way, two men ran up, attacked, and beat them. Lilburn collapsed under the attack and lay in a pool of his own blood. He'd received repeated blows to his head. His briefcase contained cash, and his perpetrators ran off with it. A passerby happened upon them and called the police. Lilburn never regained consciousness and was pronounced dead the next day in the hospital. He was buried in Sterkfontein Cemetery, outside

Krugersdorp, near their home.

This is a story I've heard all my life because it is the story of my own grandparents. Lilburn Adkins was my mother's father. Though he died before I was born, his story has always been a part of my history. At this point, I know more about his death than his life. I knew he lived, worked, was killed, and buried in South Africa. I have always felt a distance from those events, and from deeply knowing his story. Now, I found myself as a photographer and educator included in a fellowship to convene in South Africa, joining other artists from all over Africa, the U.S. and Canada, to study and make work about this fascinating and complex country. I was also on a mission to visit Lilburn Adkins' grave.

Deep Undertones

South African author, Alan Paton, who wrote the seminal 1948 novel *Cry, The Beloved Country* said of his home that, "When one thinks of it and remembers it, one is aware…of solemn and deep undertones that have nothing to do with any mountain or any valley, but have to do with men."

From my own experience there, I saw and felt these undertones in South Africans from all walks of life. I grappled with a way to understand their struggles, seeing first-hand the results of sometimes senseless retribution. It was all more overwhelmingly complex than I had thought. What I came home with, besides a refreshed appreciation for all that I take for granted, was a realization that the struggles South Africans experience are *everyone's* struggles. Their successes, failures and attempts to engender hope and equality can be seen as a microcosm of the larger human condition: what we all want we can't have… yet.

I had never previously set foot on the African continent, and was not equipped to associate, much less integrate South

Africa with the most important parts of my life. Perhaps my not wanting the past to dominate or define my experience, and the lack of first-hand exposure to the continent had done Africa a disservice for me. I saw that I had my own colonialist ideas about this place that was too many times referred to as merely a "mission field," which, whether I knew it or not, downgraded its culture and history to just a backdrop for the stories. It was where my mother was born, and my grandfather was buried; where many cousins and friends grew up or worked; the subject of countless stories that colored my view. I remember Bono championing an awareness of and resistance to Apartheid. I could recall vague reports of Nelson Mandela getting released from a prison to become their president...but I possessed little understanding of the significance of these events.

While I was excited about going on this trip, these misunderstandings and foggy, inaccurate perspectives spawned performance anxiety and imposter syndrome...fear about whether I could engage with what we would encounter, and hold my own as part of a group of artists that were, I felt, much more impressive and promising than I. It dredged up the shame of being the new kid, having moved a lot, and always being 'different'. The shame and insecurities did not just feel exposed but magnified—pulling me inward like hypothermic reaction to extreme cold. I left the U.S. for Johannesburg full of my own internal tension, wondering if this opportunity would be worth leaving my family for two weeks. I felt the pressure to make the most of it, though I had little idea of what to expect, and less inspiration from which to draw. In short, I felt completely alone.

The Queens of Soweto by Keith A. Barker. 2013. Silver gelatin print. • These women sat proudly for me after mass at the Regina Mundi Church in Soweto, the site for many anti-Apartheid demonstrations and activities, most notable of which was a violent clash with police in the 1977. Though no one was killed in that skirmish, the church building still bears scars of bullet holes fired within the church.

Tension

> *Why do you show me iniquity,*
> *And cause me to see trouble?*
> *For plundering and violence are before me;*
> *There is strife, and contention arises.*

The trip took our group mainly to Johannesburg, Pretoria, and Cape Town. Hearing first-hand stories and histories from so many varied perspectives, I felt myself gaining a richer view of South Africa's past and present. A more accurate color and focus came to all the distant knowledge I'd possessed. I came to realize that the nation is like life itself: it is full of dichotomous tension. I could relate with tension; I was feeling it.

South Africa, I was told, is where the best humankind can offer is set right next to the absolute worst. This young nation has a centuries-long story of rich culture. It is a melting pot of languages, ethnicities, cultures, and people groups, yet has become synonymous with slavery, unmitigated bigotry, and racial violence. It is the wealthiest and most developed of any nation in the continent yet shows equal extremes of poverty and need, along with pervasive extortion and corruption. Yet I am not immune to culpability: the retrieval of resources that make my life easier is at the expense of the poor and destitute. The computer on which I type, the phone I use every day, the platinum and silver I sometimes use for photographic emulsions, not to mention the fact that they mine gold and diamonds there...all materials extracted from this very human landscape.

Some tensions might be unique to the country but contain characteristics common to the collective human experience. Many South Africans I encountered—painters, philanthropists, priests, professors, and poets—recounted personal experiences and perspectives of their homeland. I found myself identifying with much of the content of their stories, because I realized they embody our common human story.

The tensions and insecurities in my own life were put in perspective by my being awakened to situations I was unable to know first-hand. We saw the profound natural beauty of the land—something I missed in all the stories I had heard. We visited an HIV/AIDS support group full of very happy, hopeful people, though their realities were foreign and sobering to me. We walked through muddy shantytowns where the poorest lived, and yet saw everywhere how artforms of every imaginable expression, such as tapestries, sculptures, music, paintings, and photographs were what helped them express what they endured, felt, and remembered.

We heard stories from still-displaced former residents of

District Six in Cape Town—a place known for racial oppression and suffering. Over a twenty-two-year period, thousands of law-abiding citizens were forcibly removed from their homes in the district by Apartheid power, solely due to the skin color and multi-racial lineage of the residents. Yet, those to whom we spoke, passed on their stories in hopes of keeping the memories and realities alive. We experienced memorials, monuments and sacred places designed to help us remember the events, people, and traditions that went before.

Sterkfontein Cemetery by Keith A. Barker • One of the photographs taken at Lilburn Adkins' grave site.

Part of the Story

"...The only power which can resist the power of fear is the power of love. It's a weak thing and a tender thing; men despise and deride it. But I look for the day when in South Africa we shall realize that this only lasting and worth-while solution of our grave and profound problems lies not in the use of power, but in that understanding and compassion without which human life is an intolerable bondage…"

When I got into that little red Audi, it was not lost on me that I was at the mercy of a stranger in a foreign land in which I was a minority. But the hour-long drive to the other side of Johannesburg allowed for a chance to get to know my driver. Tumi shared his perspectives on things, and I learned a lot. As we traveled, the early morning sun slid warm light across the landscape.

It occurred to me that I should communicate to my guide the expectations I had about what would happen once we found the grave. I am a photographer; I knew that I could take at least 20–30 minutes to photograph but…my stomach dropped. I suddenly realized how ill-prepared I was. I didn't know what would happen next. Do I just stand there? Take a hundred pictures of the tombstone?

When we got to the gate of the cemetery, Tumi seemed as relieved as I, and had a couple of conversations with the cemetery caretaker in a dialect incomprehensible to me. Cleared to drive in, we began looking for the gravesite. The organization of the plots reflected the color of skin. Racial segregation accompanies Africans even to their graves, I realized.

We followed the caretaker, zigzagging back and forth until we found Section 3, and searched for plot M-64. I found it:

LILBURN EDWARD ADKINS
FAITHFUL UNTO DEATH.

Everything about the grave seemed somehow different than the few pictures I had seen. I wondered: *Why did I even come? Was this all a waste of time?* The morning light did make it beautiful. I stood there and looked at a low, granite stone with the name, dates, and abrupt epitaph; the stone slabs delineating the plot; the small pebble-gravel spread over the rectangle of earth where the casket was lowered decades before. Over sixty years of life distilled to a granite marker. No fanfare, no lightning bolts, nothing out of the ordinary; only silence and a soft breeze on a hillside overlooking a beautiful view to the East.

Tumi quietly walked up and broke into my thoughts. "Sometimes when African people come to see a grave, they clean it up a bit." He suggested we pull some of the weeds that had grown up through the pebbly, white gravel that marked the rectangular grave, and he produced a tire iron from the car which we used to pull, dig, and scrape. A little embarrassed, it dawned on me how much more humbling my actions ended up being at the grave side. Plus, I thought, *anyone*, not just Africans wanting to honor the dead, should want to dress things up a bit. "A nice gravesite makes it look like the person buried there is still remembered," Tumi said. He was right.

I grabbed three small pebbles from the plot and put them in my pocket. It felt a little like stealing, and a little like the right thing to do.

On the way home, I thought about the purpose of it all. I guess feeling some need to justify all the fuss of this side-trip, I found myself expressing how it seemed significant for me to visit the grave even though I didn't personally know my own grandfather. Tumi said, "Now *you're* part of the story!" Right again.

To Be Carried

Sculptor Dumile Feni's (1942 -1991) piece entitled *History* graces the entrance of Constitution Hill in Johannesburg, where their Chief Justices preside and uphold the South African Constitution. The bronze sculpture features an elongated, stylized human figure yoked like a mule to a cart holding two more figures. At first glance it seems to manifest the "intolerable bondage" of which Paton wrote. That interpretation makes the most sense, given the struggles with which many South Africans readily identify. However, such was not the artist's intent. We were told by the docent that Feni said of this piece, "It is about the reality that sometimes we carry, and at other times we are carried."

History (maquette 1987, bronze 2003) by Dumile Feni (1942–1991). Johannesburg, Constitutional Court Collection. Photo by Keith A. Barker.

Invisible lines divide in so many places. My friend Father Peter once told me (I found out later he was quoting Alexander Solzhenitsyn): the line between good and evil runs right through each of our hearts. Even in my small town in Kentucky, vastly different rhythms, schedules, perspectives, and expectations separate those who live in proximity. I live near people I seldom see and with whom I interact even less. Mixed in are the differing interests, ways of spending time, money and energy, and disparate convictions regarding topics like child-rearing, politics, sexual identity, sports, guns, theology, even recycling.

Sometimes harmless, sometimes not, these differences create an *otherness* that might make neighbors seem like foreigners.

I am not very good at letting others help or carry me, or at communicating my needs. Independence causes one to miss out on the riches of *inter*dependence. Feni's sculpture did not come to mind until weeks after the trip as I settled in back home with my family. We faced our share of unexpected hardships that summer like my dad's heart surgery and stroke, a deep cut on my four-year-old son's forehead requiring stitches (and a lot of screaming), my wife's hyperextended knee, my daughter's fractured foot...just to mention the physical stresses. Though they pale in comparison to the struggles of so many South Africans, especially those of color, the help and presence of many people carried us through it. Feni's humble bronze sculpture spoke to me long after the trip. The thought of sometimes having to be carried became more poignant, human, and real. Our little family needed the help. Letting people help us continues to be part of our healing process.

Struggle creates human need, as well as a moment of opportunity to carry others and to be carried. In my mind I drift back to the early 1960s where I imagine my grandparents living and thriving, carrying, and being carried among their friends in Krugersdorp. I know they rubbed elbows with a few of the thousands of miners who were laboring in inhuman and dangerous conditions far below the high veldt. Did my grandparents know in that same moment of history that sixty-nine unarmed civilians were shot and killed by white police in what became known as the Sharpeville Massacre? Could they have known about an activist named Nelson Mandela who publicly and defiantly burned the passbook that he and all South African blacks were required to carry under Apartheid law? Tensions were high. This was as volatile a time as any in that country's history. Of course they knew, but I still wonder:

what were my grandparents *doing* in such a dangerous place, anyhow? How did all those tensions affect them? Did they have friends, or did they feel alone? Did they help carry those around them? How were they carried? If they were there to do good, why were they subjected to such brutal suffering and even death?

The answers to those questions are lost to history. Asking them is part of what it means to be human. My grandparents' lives and my grandfather's death are part of that country's story. I can see my own story in light of my grandfather's. It's all a grand, complex story, with meaning, structure, and purpose if I'm looking. Just like Feni's sculpture, the narrative is not just a concrete depiction of reality; there's room for interpretation, for grace, for humanity. I could not feel my grandfather's pain, or weep at his grave because his life was full of moments I can never share or know. There's room for all we don't and cannot know. The topic and theme are too big for words. Just like my trip to this country was too big for photographs, Lilburn's life *was* bigger than his gravesite.

Past and future are inextricably related, and the locus, the crux, the point of contact is this present moment in time. I think Father Brown's assertion that we are on the wrong side of the tapestry means somewhere else, on the other side, we will know as we are known. It will somehow make sense.

Until then I will hang on to those three small pebbles.

Endnotes

1. G.K. Chesterton. *The Innocence of Father Brown.* "The Sins of Prince Saradine." Andrews UK Ltd. 2010. pp. 125–6.
2. Florence's injuries required many days of hospitalization, and though she did recover, she was unable to attend her husband's funerals. There were two services conducted due to segregation; one for the whites and one for the workers in the

mining camp where they had been working—many of those people were from Mozambique.

3. Lewis Gannett quoting Alan Paton from Gannett's introduction to the 1959 Scribner's edition.

4. Habakkuk 1:3

5. From Cry, The Beloved Country. Lewis Gannett quoting Alan Paton; from Gannett's introduction to the 1959 Scribner's edition. p. xix

6. Brené Brown writes, "Somehow, we have come to equate success with not needing anyone. A similar line divides us when help is needed. We've divided the world into 'those who offer help' and 'those who need help.' The truth is that we are both." Brown, Brené. The Gifts of Imperfection: Let Go of Who You Think You're Supposed to Be, and Embrace Who You Are. Hazelden. 2010. p, 20.

Keith A. Barker's photography centers around people, places and objects that relay a sense of history and memory. Barker has taught Photography in the Art and Design Department at Asbury University since 2000, and holds a Master of Fine Arts in Photography from Savannah College of Art and Design. Besides hiking the woods near his home, he enjoys trail running, listening to music, splitting wood, and playing outdoors with his family in central Kentucky. More of his photographs can be seen at www.kabarker.art

Just You and I

Angela B. Curnutt

(content warning: this story includes references to domestic violence.)

As a cradle Catholic, I always knew you needed your faith to do what needs to be done to get to Heaven, however when I was a young adult, I didn't put much thought or action into this. I was drinking, going out to clubs on a Saturday night, making it home around four to five in the early Sunday morning and forgetting to go to Mass. In my defense, I would have gone if my head didn't hit the sofa pillows, and my fluffy pink throw didn't somehow make it half way on my body. In the back of my head, I always knew once you got to a certain adult age, you quit all the foolishness, running around with whomever, whenever. Reluctantly, limiting your sins is what you did to get right with Jesus. A lot of my friends put their faith aside, and some decided to lose it on purpose. I saw their lives from the outside looking in and it didn't appear so bad. My mother always warned me, "If you don't stop that foolishness, God will stop you." Deep down I knew she was right, but I ignored it just for a few more moments.

A few unmonitored moments turned into a few years, then I met a man by the name of Mark Benjamin. He was dashing at a stocky five foot, two inches tall, dark hair with a touch of gray at his temples, semi-droopy dark eyes, with an elaborate set of verbal skills that would melt the cheese right into your egg and bacon taco. He eloquently spoke with his encyclopedic words with a touch of street lingo. He would literally give you the brown flannel shirt off his back. On one cold afternoon, coming out of the grocery store right where the warmth of your surroundings turns into the wintery air from the outside, a young man in his late teens to early twenties suffered a seizure and dropped directly in front of us. Mark right away took off his brown flannel shirt to use it as a pillow. He held the hand of that young man so his mom could contact the ambulance. Mark watched him have that thirty second seizure all while whispering, "You're going to be ok. It will pass. All this will pass." Mark always used those words; it was his life mantra. Once the ambulance arrived, we stepped aside so the medics could do their due diligence. The young man's mother picked up Mark's shirt, presented it to him. "Thank you for your kindness, sir."

Mark was no stranger to strangers. He spoke and interacted with everyone. This must have been where the first attraction was, other than the looks. Both of us being Leos, it was a bit difficult at times, but we made it work. Our personalities were strong and equal. Things were unlike what I was previously used to in my relationships. Mark was fourteen years my senior. Being twenty-four never felt so good, until it felt like pain.

Mark promoted me from girlfriend to wife in a matter of moments after meeting me, although he always told me a marriage doesn't mean a piece of paper. I never knew how to be a proper housewife, and Mark had some outmoded ideas of what our lives would be like. I stayed home while he worked. I was expected to be at home and not leave. I persuaded myself to believe it's not all that bad. No children, just me, alone, until the evenings. I remember the early hours of September 19, 1997, when he came home drunk, which was something he often did. It was my understanding that real men did what they wanted and to hell with the women who are left behind. This is the part I have always wanted to forget. I simply can't forget. I define these moments as deep life stains. There were so many stains. This one in particular went like this. I was furious that he would leave me home by myself as he went off to have a good time. Weren't we a couple? Weren't we supposed to go do things together? For an aging vato stuck in the 1970s lowrider-esque era, I guess not. Besides, he told me we were married, he didn't need a piece of paper. This was an accepted absurdity on my part. I didn't let him enter the house. I questioned his whereabouts, his cohorts, his actions and his excuses. He violently replied with a right hook to my face. Falling down on my back, I hit the concrete steps leading to the back door. I screamed. This was just the beginning. As I cried for mercy, he grabbed the top of my hair and threw me to the ground. I landed face down with a mouth full of small pebbles and dirt. I planted my palms on each side of me to get up, and his steel toe boot smashed my left hand. Screaming for him to let go, he was equally screaming, "You will never question me again! Do you hear me?" He then made sure I heard him. There was no more Angela in me, but there was plenty of Mark left in him. I made it to a kneeling position; he picked me up just to throw me down again. After, he went inside to go to bed. I used my good arm to army crawl into the house, like a slug leaves its slime trail, I too left my trail of blood. I pulled myself slowly and made it to the bedroom. My adrenaline was quickly diminishing. I made it to the closet door and closed my eyes.

"WHAT THE HELL HAPPENED TO YOU!" Mark yelled at me. I couldn't move, my body was sore. My natural reaction was to open my eyes properly, but I couldn't.

"Angela, what happened to you? Who did this to you?" he asked.

"What?" I replied in disbelief.

Right away he put both arms under mine to pick me up from the floor.

"Stop, you're hurting me!" I replied loudly.

"I'm sorry, baby, I'll get you to the bed," he answered.

On the wall above the dresser was an oval mirror. I saw the reflection, but I didn't see me. I saw Mark assisting someone. If you looked from afar, it appeared heroic. Someone carrying a physically depleted person from battle. I could feel his very muscular arms around my body guiding me to the bed. Who was that lion? The black and purple swollen forehead gross fully protruding, a smashed large nose covered in dry blood, two black eyes, the white of my left eye red, several gash lines on each side of my face. The purple handprint across my neck with several pronounced bruises covering my chest. The distal phalanges on my left ring finger will never go straight again. The blood-covered, poor, defeated lion in the mirror was me.

Mark laid me down on the bed. "How did this happen?" He sounded genuine. Crying, I immediately replied hatefully, "It was you! How could you do this to me?" "But it wasn't me! I would never hurt you... I love you!" he replied.

My tears just gushed out like the destruction of a dam. Instantly my head started to throb, my body ached, I wanted to go home. I didn't want to be there. I needed to stop crying because I ached, but I couldn't help it. Mark put on his emotionally-driven medic uniform to collect all the first aid supplies he could locate. He came back to doctor me up. I never went to the emergency room. He allowed me to sleep the rest of the day. I slept for about ten hours. I still remember the reflection of the defeated lion, the sting of the alcohol he used to erase the blood stains to my upper body, the look of regret on his face. If you didn't know us, you might call the scene a romantic one which the man comes to the rescue of the woman he loves. I called it venomous. To this day when I stretch out my left hand extending my fingers, all comply except the deformed ring finger.

Don't get me wrong, Mark wasn't a two or three times a week violator. He was more like the debt collector, trying to collect once a month. I remember another time much later in our "marriage" when we started arguing about who we are, where is this relationship going, I'm going to leave... the normal threat. I started to ask questions he wasn't too keen on answering. He headed out the door with his truck keys. So what would any respectable battered wife do... follow him... yep, right out the door into the front yard. My mother would call it por cabezuda, which translates to basically hardheaded. I would call it toxic at its finest. Out in the yard, we argued for all the neighbors to see. He finally got tired of listening, so I got violently pushed into a Y-shaped tree. Falling backwards, my left leg was caught between the branches that formed the Y shape. I turned my body to catch my fall. Many years later, when I sprained my left knee exercising, the doctor asked me how long it had taken for my torn ACL to heal. It was plain as day on my MRI. Eyes wide open!

So let's get back to coming to Jesus. I am a firm believer in holy water. I keep it everywhere. I have used it twice to save my life. One night Mark came home drunk, again. I was angry, but not lion angry. I went into the kitchen to confront him about his responsibilities. Right away he put his hand over my mouth and told me, "Go...get to bed and get comfortable, I'm going to whip your ass when I get in there."

I acted as if I wasn't scared, but inside I was scared and trembling. I went back to the bedroom, used my time to quickly and frantically search for the bottle of holy water. I quietly opened all dresser drawers, moving all their contents, panicking that I wouldn't find it. I knew Mark would destroy me for being a smart ass. Quickly, I looked in the nightstand drawer and there it was. I placed the small one-ounce plastic bottle I got from San Juan Basilica in my hand, and turned off the lights to act as if I was asleep. I could see the lights from the kitchen from under the bedroom door. I then saw the lights turn off and heard footsteps approaching. Mark opened the door to the bedroom and walked towards me. I could barely make out his face in the shadows. Instantaneously I took the holy water, poured some in my palm and recited, "In the Name of God the Father, God the Son and God the Holy Spirit, leave me alone!"

Mark froze. A sinister voice exclaimed, "Don't put that stuff on me!"

He then plunged into the bed. I laid there in the bed and prayed. I knew enough to know, spiritually speaking, I couldn't continue this. Not only was I living in sin with a man who didn't want to marry me legally, but I couldn't even pretend it was my best life. This had to stop. I prayed for God to save me. I prayed for my confused cluttered mind, I prayed for the intelligence that I was obviously lacking. I looked out the window to the sky, begging for life. I saw a plane and wished I was a passenger on that plane. I cried in silence; I didn't want to wake him. I just laid there gripping the holy water tightly.

After some time went by, we looked like a normal

couple. We didn't have children together. We could always do what we wanted. We didn't require much money, small grocery lists would suffice, going out to dinner with friends was what we did. We went to breakfast at a small diner. We bickered about something, but for a while I refused to look at him.

"Babe, it's not my fault," he whispered.

I turned around to see his smile, he was pointing at his plate. Ordering waffles was part of his plan all along. The man cut out a letter "A" in his waffle. I couldn't help it, I started laughing. He smiled and said, "A for Angela, A for Angel, A for Asshole that I am."

Sometime later Mark took me to Sacred Heart Catholic Church, in front of The Blessed Mother statue he kneeled and asked me to kneel beside him. He vowed right there, in front of Our Lady, that he would never beat me up again. I believed him because at that point it had been over two years since our last episode.

"I want to marry you, in a Catholic church," he said. "I want you to belong to me and I want God to bless us."

During the course of a year, he had one-on-one appointments with Father Raphael in order to fully prepare us to get married by church. When November 2008 came, I was ready to be married. It was the traditional Mexican wedding complete with a mass, the mariachi band singing the mass, the reception, with the mariachi band playing during the course of the dinner, and the dance. Even when the mariachi band left, we kept singing mariachi songs.

When the court of honor took the spotlight to be introduced, they walked into the hall to the song, "When a Man Loves a Woman" by Percy Sledge. However, when the new Mr. & Mrs. came through, you would think another romantic song would play to express our love. Nope, we walked in dancing, through our own Soul Train line, to "Lowrider" by War. We had a blast! It was many years since the first time we became a couple. To me it was worth it.

Later that year, Mark decided to register for RCIA classes (Rite of Christian Initiation for Adults), those are the classes one takes to either 1: convert catholic or 2: make the sacraments you didn't when you grew up. He had never made his first communion and confirmation.

I felt as if our past was just a really bad nightmare. Mark was completely different. He kept his word to me. It seemed as if he was trying to make up for our lost time. Saturdays were always the same. Mark did yard work while I cleaned the house. One fall Saturday, Mark went to rake the yard. The raking was necessary because we had two huge pecan trees and some smaller trees that towered over the roof of the house. Inside I turned on the stereo to some good house cleaning music and went to town.

"Babe, come here please," he requested.

"Ok one second," I replied.

I went to the fridge to pull out a bottle of water. I knew he would be thirsty. I made my way out the back sliding doors through the patio into the backyard.

"What are you doing up there?" I asked curiously

"I want you to see something, come climb up this ladder."

I wondered what he wanted to show me. He climbed down the ladder, so I climbed up. "Please hold the ladder, don't let me fall."

He responded with a smile, "Now look to your left."

"Oh, wow!" He had actually raked all the leaves into the shape of an A-N-G-E-L-A. I laughed.

"It's because I love you, Angela!" Mark said with smile overload.

I felt it. Right away I climbed down to get my phone for

a photo. I took two photos of the yard. This man here loves me enough to rake up the leaves to shape my name. Yep, how many can say that?

He was always doing little things to make me smile. Buying corn dogs at the pier in Galveston, he used the mustard to spell out my name. Or when we went to the art supplies store, he used the test markers section to draw my name onto the blank drawing pad. Mark had a talent for drawing, and he used it on my name. He certainly was the love of my life.

One day we were discussing children. We were not getting pregnant. We never used protection nor was I on contraceptives. We decided to go seek medical assistance. After many tests, labs, and exams, it was determined I could never conceive. I was diagnosed with polycystic ovarian syndrome. My body didn't make enough hormones to conceive a child. This would explain the lack of menstrual cycles and those cycles that would last into the next month. After the last doctor's appointment, Mark took me to the church. We both kneeled in front of the tabernacle. In front of God Himself, I sobbed and begged Him to give me a child. I continued to explain how everyone was having children, those that are much younger than me. I went on to explain how I wanted to leave a legacy. When I should pass, my wish was to be surrounded by my children and grandchildren. The best compliment I could hear was someone telling my children, "You look exactly like your mother."

How I wanted that more than anything. I was so hurt and devastated. All I did was cry and try to speak clearly. I prayed, "Please Father in Heaven, please don't forget me. Please don't forget to give me children." I put my head down so no one would see my face. Mark put his hand on my shoulder to console my tears. I understood if it's not God's will for me to have children it just wouldn't be. I had to make peace with that thought in my heart. After about half an hour, we went home. I left the church with a touch of hope.

As good as life is, it can change quickly and dramatically. About a year had passed by when I heard Mark say, "Babe, I need to go to the hospital."

I reached for the lamp on the nightstand to turn it on. I found Mark laying down on his side of the bed with his hand pressing against the right side of his abdomen. He was the never-go-to-the doctor type. His joke about his ailments was "Just walk it off." I knew it in my gut, if he's asking to go to the emergency room then it's serious. I jumped up to change and put my hair in a ponytail. Mark, on the other hand, could not move so easily. I collected his sweats and a t-shirt to assist him in changing.

We drove down to the hospital. Mark was triaged right away. It was 5:30 am September 8, 2010. He was quickly administered pain medication, which took effect right away. Mark once again was calm. We talked all day, laughed about events in our past. I made fun of him saying this was his extensive plan to get out of work while he made fun of my fashion sense, considering I put my shirt on backwards and inside out, a double whammy.

"Babe," he said in a low somber tone. "I just want you to know I love you, I always loved you." I knew it right when he started speaking that something wasn't right. What was going on?

"I'm sorry for ever putting my hands on you," he said while his eyes looked down in shame. This was not the time to argue, to make corrections or to confirm what he said. My faith taught me this was the apparent time to listen, but most importantly, to tell him that I loved him very much. It would be a few months before I would say the words, "I forgive you." But I did, I just wouldn't say it at first.

"I'm going to find some coffee; I need to wake up," I told him.

"Ok, I'll be right here," he responded.

Dejected and sorrowful, I sought out solace and found coffee to gather myself.

All day we conversed extensively, even played the "If I won the lottery what would I do" game. We kept each other occupied. The nurses would come periodically to ask for more blood work, a specimen here and there, another round of imaging. Mark complied. I could see the seriousness in his face. Mark was gifted with a significant amount of will along with an abundance of determination. In retrospect, when he made the promise to never get violent with me again, he also promised to give up drinking entirely every other year for a complete year. Everyone was surprised, but of course there's always that one person tempting him with money so he would drink.

"Mark, I'll give you this fifty-dollar bill if you drink with me," they proposed.

Mark politely responded, "Yes, I need that money, but no, I won't accept your challenge." He referred to those dry years as his boring years, then that big smile on his face would project like sunlight. He always had the biggest most fun smile.

"Mr. & Mrs., I've been overseeing your complete evaluation, I'm the doctor on call here at the hospital," the doctor informed us. "Let's go sit in the conference room, follow me." The doctor appeared to be concerned, which freaked me out, but I kept silent.

"Please have a seat." The doctor pointed at the seats, he then sat across from us at the table.

"Is this the results of all my exams?" Mark asked.

"Yes sir, let me explain our findings," the doctor responded.

The rest of the time was a blur in my memory. We were

told Mark had stage four liver cancer. Due to his bilirubin being so high, it was suggested our options for combatting the disease were few to none. My heart instantly broke into a million little pieces. I bargained with God. "Please don't take him from me." I could see it in his face, Mark was doing his own bargaining. A lot of our memories came to the front of my memory bank. For example, deciding to go to Galveston to fish at 10:30 pm on a Friday late evening. Then watching the sunrise from the 61st pier the next morning and feeling gratitude to God for the thoughtful creation of spectacular beauty. On the way home, Mark contemplating if we should stop at the local grocery store seafood department to pick up the biggest fish and conjure up the greatest tale of fish defeat. Or the time when we picked up searing hot French fries at the drive through and drove away. In order to cool them down, I opened the small bag of fries placing them out the window to cool just for them to get blown all away. I admit it, at times we were plain run-of-the-mill weirdos.

The first oncology appointment consisted of what we feared the most: no hope.

"Mr., we are going to review your tests, we will call you tonight with the results," the nurses told us.

We got home and continued our everyday routine. We prepared dinner, set the table and ate. "Angela, I want you to promise me something," Mark said.

"What?" I replied.

"I want you to promise me you will never get with anyone like me, not even my friends. I want you to get with someone that will buy you things I couldn't, to get with someone who will take you places I couldn't, I want you to have a life I couldn't provide for you, but mostly I want you to get with someone who will never hit you."

I looked down to cry. I rushed out the room, I didn't want him seeing me bawl like a baby. The phone rang just in time to rip us from that grievous moment.

"Hello." Mark answered the phone on speaker so we could both hear.

"Mark Benjamin?" the caller asked.

"Yes, this is me," he confirmed.

"I wanted to inform you about your test results," she said. "Your bilirubin has tripled since the day you presented to the emergency room, which was five days ago. This cancer is fierce," she exclaimed.

Mark cleared his throat to speak. "Let me ask you, just tell me plain, how long do I have?"

The caller hesitantly proceeded, she also had to clear her throat, then after five seconds she answered, "About six months to a year I would say."

"Ok thank you very much." He hung up the phone. "I want to be left alone for a few minutes Angela, if I can, please."

"Of course," I responded. We lived two houses down from my aunt so I ran to her house, my cousin was there I grabbed him. "He's dying! Mark is dying!" I hugged my cousin hard. He reciprocated while I screamed, "Mark is dying!"

My cousin whispered, "I know mama, I know, you will get through this, I promise." He kissed the top of my head. "I promise."

The next day Mark and I saw a commercial for a hospital that specialized in cancer treatment. It wasn't in town; it was in another state, actually. "Let's call them," he said.

I did what he told me. Within a week's time we were boarding a plane, Arizona bound. We arrived at Sky Harbor International Airport in Phoenix. At baggage pick up, there was a man wearing a chauffeur type uniform holding a sign which indicated the hospital name as well as our last name. Mark and I both looked at each other to hold in the laugh. We were escorted to the limousine. On the way to the hospital, we witnessed magnificence: the mountain ranges were so majestic, very appealing to the peaceful senses. The scenery was very unfamiliar to us compared to flat Houston.

The hospital campus was gorgeous from top to bottom. The lobby greeted you with light gray carpet, color matched large sofas with recliners. A light brown brick accent wall with fireplace and wood mantel. A service desk, entrance to a dining hall with huge coffee and infused water urns. In the background there was a violin player playing for guests, and a baby grand piano down the hall you could play whenever you want. Down the main hall there was a pharmacy, across from the pharmacy was a store and gift shop attached to a coffee shop that specialized in natural smoothies, and the hall to the right included offices and lobbies fit for all your medical appointments. We checked in at the service desk while our luggage was shuttled to our room.

"Lunch begins at 11:00 am," the kind gentleman informed us.

The oncology team did not hesitate. They recommended a strong dose of chemotherapy, but first surgery was needed to insert a port into Mark's chest for easy chemo application. Mark started his therapy eight hours a day, five days a week. It had been proven the chemo therapy was working. The biggest tumor was the size of a quarter, but shrank to just a bit bigger than a nickel.

For the next two months, we returned to the hospital the last week of the month. Considering Mark was going through this horrible disease, he always maintained his energy, positive thought process and faith. The hospital made it possible for us to attend mass and go to confession at the local Catholic church. That year we celebrated Thanksgiving at the hospital with our new friends. Later that week I noticed, for the first time, Mark appeared a bit more tired. We would walk into the cotton fields behind the hospital to talk, but this time he didn't want to walk. We sat outside in the patio to stare toward the Estrella mountains. We didn't talk we just held hands. We knew what we were both thinking.

"Angela, I need to tell you something," Mark said.

"Ok," I replied.

"I'm not going to be here for Christmas," he said in a quiet voice. He tightened his grip of my hand. "I want you to know this. I feel it. I don't know why I feel it, but I do," he said in a depressed tone.

"Don't say that, please don't tell me that," I begged, holding back tears.

"I have to go to the restroom," he told me.

I looked into the sky and prayed, "Please Father in Heaven, please give me the strength to endure what is to come."

We returned home. Landing back in Houston, we saw elaborate Christmas decorations. Mark loved Christmas, his favorite holiday. Normally we would celebrate by taking a Christmas tour of houselights. Since we really couldn't afford the increased light bill during the season, we drove into the well-to-do neighborhoods to marvel at the houses that could. It was fun touring houses that went all out this time of year. We played "guess what type of work they do to afford all the lights." We had it narrowed down to doctor, high priced lawyer, CEO, CFO, and drug dealer. Afterwards we would go home, drink hot chocolate and eat dulce or sweet bread. We sat in silence in the living room.

"I see cartoons," Mark woke me up.

"What?" I asked confused. I instantly opened my eyes to look at the clock showing 3:15 am.

"I see cartoons, not like Tom and Jerry or Mickey Mouse, I see everything white," he continued.

Immediately I turned on the lamp. Mark was laying

down with his eyes closed talking. "God, if you're going to take me, I'm ready, but please take care of my Angela," he prayed out loud.

"What do you see?" I asked.

"Everything is shiny white," he explained.

I got out of bed, dropped to my knees in panic and prayed, "Dear Father in Heaven, please don't let Mark suffer. If you are going to take him, please hear my prayer, don't let him suffer."

The time was now. The oncologist made his routine weekly visit. It was recommended a hospice facility would be better equipped for palliative care. That late morning an ambulance arrived to take Mark to hospice. I grabbed a few items. We arrived, greeted by a team of empathetic professionals. The nurses took charge of us, handling everything that was needed. We were taken to our room. It was a cozy bed-and-breakfast type of setting complete with a hospital bed dressed like no other, two recliners with a sofa, along with a beautiful Afghan blanket draped in the back and a tv mounted on the wall. To the left of the bed there were bookshelves filled with books, puzzles, and magazines.

All this time, I never saw or heard Mark get upset about being diagnosed. His spirit was tough. He was in full peaceful acceptance of what was to come. The nurses applied an additional catheter and that's when I heard an exhausted loud voice pleading for mercy.

"It hurts!" he yelled. I grabbed a pillow from the sofa to release my sadness and screamed into it. My heart couldn't stand it.

The nurse sat next to me on the sofa. She told me Mark was in the transition phase of life. She described it as one foot being in this world and the other in the next. Mark slept deep with irregular breathing. There was nothing for me to do, but

I wanted to be close to his bed. Mark opened his eyes as if it was demanded of him, he brought himself to his knees on top of the bed. He pulled off his sheets, removed his gown and nose tubing, as well as started to pull on both catheters. On his knees, he pointed towards the crown molding of the ceiling with his right hand, then lifted his left hand extending both hands like a baby boy wanting to get carried by his father.

I got scared, but something allowed me to not panic. The episode lasted one to three minutes. I saw joy on Mark's face. I have never seen joy like that before. I placed my hand on his shoulder. He turned his head towards me. He proceeded to tell me exactly who he saw, unfortunately his tongue was majorly swollen so I didn't understand what he was saying, but my heart knew.

The nurse came in to administer pain medication. "Let me check his vital signs first," she said. She checked then put down her stethoscope. "I'm sorry Mrs., it's time, we are talking minutes."

Mark laid there with both arms at his side. I grabbed his right hand. I caressed his hair backwards whispering to him, "Please don't forget me. I love you, Mark, I always have and I forgive you. Please know I forgive you," I continued. Using all the strength God supplied me, I used it not to cry. I didn't want Mark to hear me cry.

Still holding his hand I kept on repeating, "I love you, I love you, I love you." I leaned in to give him a kiss and he pursed his lips to reciprocate.

"Did you see that!" the nurse exclaimed. "He wasn't supposed to do that, he doesn't have the capability to kiss you." She was amazed.

I released his hand and took one step back. Mark breathed in and exhaled slowly; his life was over. It was time to face it, my life was over too. There was no returning from this darkness. I grabbed the pillow and screamed a well needed louder than life scream. "Where are you?" I yelled into the pillow. "Why did you leave me? Take me with you, I'm going to be alone! Don't leave me, please take me with you! Because of you, I'm never going to be a mother, never going to be a wife again! Why!" I yelled as loud as I could get. "My life is over!"

I closed my eyes and envisioned the devil himself in front of me. That demonic evil punched a hole into my chest to yank out my once beautiful heart. He shredded it into tiny pieces. Laughing, looking at me like victory, he placed it back into my chest.

"Try to love again with this damaged heart, I bet you won't," I heard.

The nurse called my name, "You ok, honey?"

Instantly, I remembered Mark's vision. God Himself appeared to Mark to show him something grand that we as humans will never fathom. I knew Mark did not lose his soul. December 21, 2010 is the day I died...inside.

It's been almost fourteen years since the day I lost Mark. When you lose a spouse, you will never be the same ever again. It never becomes easier. You will never get over the fact your spouse is dead. Yes, you will move on, but moving on doesn't mean you forget. It's impossible to forget. Catholically speaking, I have become more aware and devoted to The Holy Souls in purgatory. I have become stronger in my faith. I recite and offer all my rosaries for Mark's soul as well as others who might be experiencing the purification before Heaven.

It brings me comfort to speak to Mark on a regular basis and write him letters. I visit his grave as well as have masses said for him. The trials God brought me through were grave ones, but He was there with me the whole way through. He never left me for one minute. I highly recommend finding your spirit. There is a world that can't be seen with the naked eye, rely on the eyes of your soul. Don't ever give up Faith, Hope and Love. This will come to pass, but it's up to us to mold the outcomes. Dear Father in Heaven, thank you for being with me; all this time I thought I was alone, but you never left. All my life, it's always been just you and I.

Angela B. Curnutt: In 2014 I married a wonderful man, Robert, and together we brought home three baby boys from the hospital. We currently live in Houston, Texas. Today, I attend St. Thomas University as a sophomore majoring in nursing with a minor in Theology. My goal is to work in hospice easing others of their potential fears and anxiety. God has provided me with trials that allowed me to obtain the tools needed and the courage to leave a high-ranking law firm to focus on my calling of helping others. This is my first professionally written story which fueled my desire to work with others. If my suffering can be the source of someone's strength then I feel that I am following the path that God has made for me.

FICTION

Ánima en Pena: Spain, 1656

Carol Zapata-Whelan

"Titles matter little. We are the children of our works."
—Don Quijote de la Mancha

Madrid, 23 de junio, 1656, Stilo Novo

As we approached the Queen's dining room, the baritone of Ánima en Pena reached us. The Queen's jester was a "son of the earth," with no father to his name. It was said he had an enchanted memory, a gift for recalling all utterances, oral or written, word for word.

Ánima en Pena, swarthy, spry, ever in his dark green suit, believed he was a soul in purgatory, punished for the sins of the fathers. Truly, the jester's penance was to torture us reciting edicts, oaths and chronicles as the spirit moved him. Like most fools, he had free rein of Palace and could do as he pleased, whether this pleased anyone else or not.

Along the Liars' Walk by San Felipe's Church, where

nobles met to gossip and craft news, some said Ánima en Pena was not a fool, but a spy, the son of a noble put to death by the Inquisition for defending secret Jews and Muslims.

But I was not at the Queen's dinner to think of such things. As a maid of honor, a *menina*, to Mariana of Austria, I had arrived at her public meal with my brother, Tadeo, to shore up my bid for a husband, the handsome younger duke, Don Julio, whose other names and titles I would add to mine the day Her Highness pledged my dowry.

At her long white table, between gilded ceilings and Persian tapestries, Queen Mariana in jeweled tresses and dark guardainfantes, wore an armor of sadness, protecting her not at all from the crushing task of producing a living heir. Neither jesters nor dwarfs nor dignitaries sparked her interest as she chewed and swallowed, young and alone. Circling her were ladies of silver hair and proud lineage: before her, the Lady of the Dish; to her left, the Lady of the Napkin; the Lady of the Drink to her right. The Queen took no wine, and drank little water, whether from Madrid's hidden springs or melted snow from the Guadarrama sierras, flavored with spices.

One thing only infused life in our Queen's gaze: her little Infanta, Margarita, whose portrait Velázquez was painting. The five-year-old princess was a small sun with cerulean eyes, bringing her own light. My role at her sittings was to lull her with English ballads I learned from my mother, whose grandfather served Felipe II in London at a time of peace.

I was pleased, if nervous, to see my brother Tadeo in his gray doublet, black eyes, black locks dancing. I was happy, too, that he had been reinstated as a page to accompany me, and that he was to serve Her Majesty's principal dish. But that dish was a foul smelling capon attracting flies. Meals of late had been poor at Palace. Merchants went unpaid for longer stretches, and even the King was reduced, at times, to dining on eggs and only eggs, preserved in ash and salt. Our wars over lands near and far were costly.

My brother and his fellow pages, all fourteen years of age, began juggling apples from a ceramic bowl. They went on to lob oranges to the jester and an Italian dwarf, Nicolás Pertusato, whose red suit shone in our room of courtiers in Spanish black per sumptuary laws. The Queen ignored her pages' poor manners and they, in turn, resisted my signals to stop.

Failing to quell the pages, I found a gilded mirror to smooth the green-blue silk of my guardainfantes over its whalebone cage. This imprisoning balloon had also been banned by sumptuary laws, but our Queen loved the fashion, so its punishing shape was *de rigeuer* at our court. At least my dress's aqua colors matched the butterfly pins on my brown wig and paired well with my eyes, my mother's own lovely blue-green eyes.

But I had little time to primp for my future husband, don Julio, as my rival cousin Urraca was soon elbowing me at the looking glass.

Urraca was in her crimson dress, a tone and cut so congenial to her Arabian eyes and figure, that I deemed myself a potted plant at her side. She was trailed by two of her minions, meninas whose endless names and titles I had not learned. They all wore the mollusk's blood paint in vogue to excess, their cheeks and collarbones caked a brick red.

Was I wearing enough paint to please the Duke?

Urraca gave me a sweetened smile, teeth bared, dark eyes hard. She feigned a curtsy—but only to take in my antiquated guardainfantes, my own dear mother's dress.

"You look—" she paused— "—*unique*, dear Doña Soledad." Her friends in blue satin skirts wide enough to wedge each in an Arc de Triomphe tittered behind pink fans.

"How is my uncle Pedro's fortune of late?" Urraca knew of my señor padre's decline and his poor luck at cards. This began when my mother failed to return home months past, on a risky errand for her Queen.

I lied that all was well and turned (rudely) to order a poem from the jester.

Anima en Pena bowed and, without introduction or preamble, recited:

"[In this year of our Lord 1492, we, Catholic Monarchs,]order all Jews and Jewesses of whatever age they may be, who live, reside, and exist in our said kingdoms and lordships, that by the end of the month of July next of the present year, they depart from all of these our said realms along with their sons and daughters, menservants and maidservants, and they shall not dare to return by penalty of death and the confiscation of all their possessions incurring these penalties by the act itself, without further trial, sentence, or declaration." *

The jester's pronouncement, from the Alhambra Decree of 1492, was quite unusual at a Queen's dinner. As the jester bowed and bounded off, I surveyed those present to judge reactions. But there seemed to be none. Courtiers in Spanish black continued their conversations. Ladies in jewel toned dresses fluttered their fans. Queen Mariana yawned at her Lady of the Napkin. The pages had moved on to juggle butter knives. My fellow maids of honor continued to trade looks and smiles with noblemen, eligible or not.

Ánima en Pena returned to me and resumed:

"And we command and forbid that any person or persons...shall dare to receive, protect, defend, nor hold publicly or secretly any Jew or Jewess beyond the date of the end of July and from henceforth forever, in their lands, houses, or in other parts of any of our said kingdoms and lordships, under pain of losing all their possessions, vassals, fortified

114

places, and [more]..." **

This edict made me think of a book my mother hid away, The Green Book, destroyed a decade past. It traced all Spanish nobles back to Sefarad, to Jewish Spain.

Again, I sought to see who listened to the jester.

Only three guests had eyes on Ánima en Pena. One was a foreign Jesuit in black, his four cornered hat under an arm; the others were Englishmen dressed in the garish colors of their nation; the younger, in green doublet and blue breeches; the elder, in yellow and red.   Drawn by their interest, Ánima bowed for the Englishmen, and in the same vein as before, proclaimed:

"Leaving Madrid this year of our Lord 1610 in the expulsion of the Muslims were one hundred and twenty-three families and of them three hundred and eighty nine persons sent back to North Africa whence their ancestors came in 711. In thanks and celebration for this success we shall have a glorious procession through Madrid and the Queen will found a new monastery."

The jester had memorized an entry I knew to be from a chronicle by León Pinelo a scribe of King Felipe III—-far from suitable entertainment for a Queen's public meal with foreign dignitaries. Before I could redirect the jester to recite a poem while the mandolin players tuned their instruments by a gold tapestry of gods in battle, I overheard the English in their tongue:

"I hold this state to be one of the most confused and disorganized in Christendom!" The older Englishman, ruddy, gray of head and beard, appeared to be confounded. "Anyone who speaks well of Spain is Catholic!"

"I am Catholic, your Grace," said the fair haired Jesuit at his side, good natured.

"Yes, but you are English!" His elder sniffed. "In *most*

matters, *unimpeachable*, my dear Antony."

I was beginning to feel the close June air in the strictures of my corset, my cheeks warm, my neck perspiring under the hot round wig. I pulled a handkerchief from my sleeve. On dabbing my face, I was horrified to see my mollusk blood paints staining the whole of the linen. And no looking glass nearby to see the state of my countenance. I stood indecisive, pulse quickening, twisting a ring on one finger, when a deep male voice behind me said in English: "Are you quite all right, your grace?"

It was the youngest Englishman (though a redhead, alarmingly handsome).

The heretic bowed, feet together English style and said his name was William Saint James. But I did not hear it. I was too intent on the state of my face and on enunciating a polite reply in English as my mother taught us—as her father taught her.

On straightening from his bow, the heretic looked—most accidentally—directly in my eyes. His were the hue of olive trees. And his face, I noted with further alarm, had suffused the color of his flaming hair.

I had never seen a human being of such a hue in all of my eighteen years in our lands, and it succeeded in distracting me in the extreme.

"I am with a friend who studied at your English seminary in Valencia, St. Alban's." He continued in his tongue. "My uncle is the English ambassador." His color was normalizing.

"The English ambassador," I repeated.

"Sir Nigel Nosworthy."

I nodded, without words in any tongue.

The heretic cleared his throat. "Sir Nigel is here as an envoy of peace."

We had been at war with lands near and far through Felipe IV's long reign thus far. And in his clearer days, my father would say: *Any Englishman seeking Peace with Spain is on a fool's errand.* Cromwell's pirates did nothing but sack our treasure fleets and attack our lands in the Indies to rob us of them. What manner of peace could one peevish ambassador hope to broker?

The heretic Englishman read my face, if not my thoughts. "Spain's interests are, indeed, opposite England's."

In this we agreed.

"Spain's end-all is to conquer more lands and souls at any cost," he informed me. "Ours is to bring peace without seeking selfish profit."

It seemed to be my turn to inform this Englishman of something. But nothing came to mind, so unaccustomed was I to such talk. My place as a maid of honor was simply to address lies or lunacy with a polite "Ah." To say "Ah" in this context amounted to treason.

It was at that instant that my brother bounded over to announce: "Our *baker* refuses to provide sweets for Her Majesty! He *says* he has *not been paid in six months!*"

Tadeo had to know that such a revelation before the English was far worse a deed than leading a herd of horses and pages into the throne room to surprise the King (for which Tadeo had been suspended until today).

Thanks to my brother's fresh impudence, the English were sure to report to Oliver Cromwell that "His Catholic Majesty" was too bankrupt to buy his wife dessert—let alone defend our Spanish Empire.

Unblinking, I unscrewed my ring and gave it to my brother. "Fast!" I hissed. "Pay the baker with this!"

Tadeo nodded—but hesitated when he saw the ring's signet.

"This one, sister?" Fear widened my brother's eyes.

The English heretic glanced at the signet ring in Tadeo's

palm.

In my haste to ready for the Queen's dinner, I had failed to exchange my mother's signet for a simpler ring and leave the heirloom in her Armada Box. I wore her ring only in our home, whenever I lost hope of seeing our mother again—and only with its signet hidden. But it was visible now. And it had been spied by a Protestant, an enemy.

Eleven months ago, our beloved Madre, Doña Pilar de Zúñiga, failed to return from a years' delayed errand for Queen Isabel, our King's first wife. My mother was bound for Sevilla, where a noblewoman, an ally, awaited a treasure she transported, an ancient book. The treasure my mother was to take to Sevilla was thought to hold a key to Peace for the People of the Book: Jews, Christians, Muslims. It was made of lead, stamped with the Seal of Solomon, held dear by the three faiths: the symbol on my mother's ring.

The tortuous history of Madre's mission has its genesis in Granada's fall of 1492, when Mohammed XII ceded Islam's last Spanish kingdom to our Catholic Monarchs, who soon banished, under pain of death, all non-Christians refusing Baptism. All Spaniards of Jewish and Islamic blood who chose to remain in their homeland were called "New Christians," *their loyalty of belief suspect*, their families ever subject to arrest, torture, death by the Inquisition. In 1609, all children of Islam, though baptized New Christians, were banished forever from Spain.

But before the banishment, a miracle, a possible reprieve: Holy relics and a parchment prophesy in Hebrew surfaced from the rubble of Granada's razed Torre Turpiana—an ancient tower built, it was thought, by a Lost Tribe of Israel. The parchment told of an Arab saint, Cecilius, bringing sacred scriptures to Spain in the time of Christ. The parchment's prophecy spoke of a lost Gospel and a Mute Book with a key to Peace. These surfaced in 1595, in Granada's caves, etched in bound lead disks,"books," inscribed in Arabic and Hebrew, stamped with Solomon's Seal.

My gifted mother, María del Pilar, her bloodlines Jewish and Muslim, had deep knowledge of Hebrew and Arabic scripts, both long forbidden. She had inherited a single lead book, a companion to the twenty-two books from Granada's caves taken to Rome for study, suspected of hoax or heresy. Before these were seized by King Felipe IV and confiscated by Pope Innocent X, they drew pilgrimages and stories of miracles. They were kept in The Secret Archive of the Four Keys at Sacromonte Abbey, where the Seal of Solomon was displayed alongside the Cross. My mother's book was thought to be a key to The Mute Book. This Mute Book, its one secret bronze copy in Sevilla, has resisted all translation. It is believed to hold a powerful prayer, a plan for peace for People of the Book—so they might live freely, on shared lands.

My mother's ring inside reads: Shalom, Salam, Paz, Peace.

But like a Sacromonte priest who never arrived at his destination on ushering the lead books to Rome, my mother never arrived in Sevilla to meet the noblewoman with the one bronze copy of the Mute Book. We yet seek our mother.

I yet feel anger at her leaving us on an impossible mission.

Was she not on a fool's errand?

"Your grace," said the redheaded Englishman, waking me from eternity in an instant of thought. "Keep your bauble."

The Protestant handed silver to my brother, who returned our mother's ring to me and rushed away for the Queen's sweets.

"*Bauble*," the Englishman had called our heirloom! And to imply Spain lacked means! I felt the blood rise in my own face.

And as Her Catholic Majesty found solace in sweets procured by a Protestant, the jester bowed and straightened to recite:

"Daily combat with enemies, cold, heat, hunger, lack of munitions, surprises everywhere, new dangers, continual deaths, until we saw that the enemy, all of them a warlike nation...vanquished, defeated, taken from their lands and dispossessed of their homes and property; prisoners, chained men and women; captive children sold in auctions or taken to live in lands far from theirs... Doubtful victory of events so dangerous, that at some point we doubted if it was us or the enemy whom God wished to punish." ***

"That is from *The War in Granada of 1610*, by Diego Hurtado de Mendoza," said my brother, astonished. "I read it to Ánima en Pena this morning."

"Your brave jester knows more than secrets by heart," said the Englishman, eyes thoughtful.

Ánima en Pena bowed again, his dark face full of light. And speaking only to those listening, the jester intoned:

The fountain's clarity is never dark
I know that all light comes from it
though it is night
So vast and fierce its currents
Such hells, such heavens and such peoples does it flood
Though it is night.

A son of the earth recited "The Dark Night of the Soul" from John of the Cross, a mystic who found God's light in the darkness of his Inquisition jail cell.

That light buried in night might yet guide me to understand my mother's sacrifice.

The lead books' Seal of Solomon repeated in my mother's

ring is twin of the Star of David. Some say the triangle's base on Earth represents the ruler's power, aiming to Heaven; and that its downturned triangle's base in Heaven is the clergy, reaching to Earth. God granted Solomon, imperfect king, a ring with the power to heal and unite in Peace.

I do not know if the lead books of Granada sparking fervor and furor in Church and State for which my mother risked all, are scriptures from Christ's time or a desperate invention of New Christians moving Heaven and Earth to remain in their homeland, to live in peace.

We continue to move Heaven and Earth to find my mother. And If the lead books she strove to decipher prove genuine, this means that Jewish and Arab families shared our lands together from the time of Christ, with full claim to citizenship in Spain. And that the Three People of the Book—Jews in Sefarad; Muslims in al-Andalus; Christians in Castilla— might follow God's light as it calls deep inside to each, to live as equals, on the same lands, in Peace.

And this is truth, I realized, even if the lead books of Granada are fictions. I learned this from a son of the earth who enforced this wisdom.

Post Script:

Don Julio, noble of many names and titles, never arrived at the Queen's dinner the night a "heretic" saved me from the Inquisition.

Though I cannot state why here, not long after, by order of the King, I was erased in "pentimento" from Velázquez's portrait of the Infanta Margarita, "La Familia de Felipe IV." It was Velázquez, of New Christian ancestors, who helped me find my mother, alive and well enough, her letters waylaid by wars, her lead book lost.

Madre, my señor padre and my brother, Tadeo, live with

us in the New World, with new names—without titles. I wear the heirloom signet always, its face to the world on a continuing errand and prayer for peace.

Shalom, Salam, Paz. Peace.

And of course: I married the Englishman.

Editor's Note: The above was translated to Modern English by an anonymous scribe in the Americas.

Author's Notes, with Informal list of Sources for further Reading:

Peace for the People of the Book is a personal, family topic for me as it was for Soledad's mother.

Anima en Pena was the self-given name of a real-life jester in Spain, a "son of the earth" ("hijo de la tierra") as children born without a father claiming paternity were unjustly called. He was thought to be the son of a noble—a spy, of privileged memory. His recitations are adapted from 1, 2, 3 below:

*1. Adapted near verbatim, The Alhambra Decreel "The 1492 Expulsion Edict of the Jews from Spain":
https://www.fau.edu/artsandletters/pjhr/chhre/pdf/hh-alhambra-1492-english.pdf

**2. Pinelo, León. Anales de Madrid de Leon Pinelo, reinado de Felipe III: Edition y estudio critico del manuscrito numero 1.255 de la Biblioteca Nacional León Pinelo, Antonio de, 1590 or 1591-1660.

***3. Historia de la guerra de Granada (1610) by Diego Hurtado de Mendoza of the powerful Mendoza family cited/translated in John Stoye, English Traveller's Abroad. Mendoza led soldiers in the war in Granada against "Moriscos," Spaniards of Islamic ancestry converted to Christianity. The violent uprisings of young men followed brutal government measures banning cultural, linguistic, religious Islamic practices, which the Catholic Monarchs, Isabel and Fernando, originally conceded in their treaty with Mohammed XII on their taking over Granada. From Philip II on, there was fear of a plotted second invasion of the Iberian Peninsula by North African forces, replicating the 711 invasion. I do not name the "enemy" in Mendoza's quoted passage. Additionally, many authors in English use the term "Moor" for the Spanish term "moro," a general term for someone of North African heritage. "Morisco" identifies "New Christian" of Islamic descent; but for respect and present day clarity of story, I say "Muslim" for those of Islamic descent in 1656 (be they "crypto-Muslims" or converts—all expelled 1609-14).

4. The English ambassador's words are taken from an earlier English ambassador to Spain during Spain and England's Pax Hispánica (1598-1621), Lord Francis Cottington (1579 – 1652). There was no English ambassador in Spain in 1656 due to spiking enmity/wars with England. The 1650 ambassador under Cromwell, Anthony Ascham, was given no quarters when he arrived in Madrid and was murdered at an inn by Irishmen said to be loyal to Charles I, but more likely loyal to Spain.

5. British historian Henry Kamen speaks of a "Green Book" destroyed in the mid 17th century, tracing all nobility in Spain to Jewish ancestry. It is also thought possible that Sephardic Jews arrived in exile in the Iberian Peninsula before the Romans extended their empire there.

6. For more on the Lead Books of Sacromonte, see the highly

informative, engagingly written The Lead Books of Granada by Cambridge scholar Elizabeth Drayson and a recent in-depth study, The Lead Books of Sacromonte and the Parchment of the Torre Turpiana: Granada, 1588-1606 by University of Amsterdam scholars, P.S. van Koningsveld and G.A.Wiegers.

7. Descriptions of poor fare in Madrid's Alcázar (palace) and, at one point, the pranks of pages at Philip IV's court have historical sources; In Avisos de Barrionuevo, "newsletter" of Philip IV, cronista Jerónimo Barrionuevo, tells of a capon with flies "stinking like dead dog" in 1656 served to the Infanta, and that the King has eaten "eggs and only eggs" at a meal. Barrionuevo also reports a Lady removing her ring to pay for sweets for the Queen when a baker refuses to send dessert due to palace payment in arrears. A courtier pays for the sweets. Barrionuevo also mentions Philip IV suspending pages on the spot for riding horses into his throne room. And at a public dinner of Mariana of Austria, a French visitor criticizes the Queen's indifference to the poor manners of pages tossing apples with a jester.

8. Diego Velázquez's iconic masterpiece "Las Meninas," originally logged in Alcázar records as "La Familia de Felipe IV," hides—as seen via Harvard imaging in the early 2000's—an unidentified young woman painted over in "pentimento" (the artist "repents"). I learned of the absented young woman after I conceived of writing from the point of view of an "erased" menina.

Carol Zapata-Whelan (PhD, UCLA) has published in *Newsweek, Hispanic Link, Brown Journal of Medical Humanities* and other periodicals to raise awareness of her son's rare genetic disorder FOP, which turns muscle to bone (IFOPA.org). She has published fiction in periodicals such as *Story Sanctum, Kaleidoscope: The Art and Language of Inclusion*, anthologies *Under the Fifth Sun: Latino Literature from California* (Santa Clara University/Heyday), *Love You to Pieces: Creative Writers on Raising a Child with Special Needs* (Beacon). Her memoir, *Finding Magic Mountain: Life with Five Glorious Kids and a Rogue Gene Called FOP* (Hachette), also appeared in Mandarin and Korean, and elicited a film in China. She is completing a YA novel, *Sol & Serafina & the A.I.R.*, about a girl who "lives" the diary of an ancestor erased from Velázquez's 1656 masterpiece Las Meninas. She teaches Spanish and Spanish American literature at California State University, Fresno.

The Mallards of St. Catherine
Zach Keali'i Murphy

Stewart came from a town where the water was abundant but never clean. Lillian came from a town where there wasn't enough water to keep the wildfires at bay.

Every Sunday morning they'd meet at a lone, wooden bench by the secluded pond at St. Catherine Trail. In the middle of the pond sprouted a fountain. On those hot days, the wind-blown mist from the glorious spout would make them feel reborn again. A set of weeping willow trees stretched over the east side of the pond, their leaves always on the verge of taking a dip. Wildflowers painted the perimeter, and sometimes Stewart and Lillian were lucky enough to see a monarch butterfly flutter by.

A flock of mallard ducks made the pond their refuge in the warmer months. It was a frenzy of wet feathers, powerful splashes, enthusiastic quacks, and deep dives. Stewart and Lillian became so familiar with the mallards that they could point out the unique quirks of each one. There was the one with the white spot on its breast that looked like a cloud. There was the one that hopped instead of waddled. And there was the one that quacked in a remarkably deep pitch that always made Stewart and Lillian laugh.

When they sat on the bench, time seemed to halt and zip by in a flash all at once. Some days there were no words needed, and other days all the words were needed. They shared what they wanted to share and left out what they wanted to leave out. Sometimes, they'd squint their eyes and see a pair of turtles poke their heads out from the pond and greet the sunshine.

Stewart and Lillian thought about carving their initials into the bench, but they ultimately concluded that it would be too cliché. They never exchanged phone numbers, for fear that it would take away the magic of their time at their sacred place. Before the winter showed its harsh might, the mallards would disappear. Stewart and Lillian would say their goodbyes, retreat from the cold, and dream of meeting at the pond once again.

As soon as the snow cleared and the ground thawed, they'd be back sitting on their beloved bench together. Shortly after, the mallards would return. Stewart and Lillian always wondered how the mallards found their way back to the same little pond after being so far away for so many moons.

One sunny March day, Stewart showed up to the bench, his face glowing with a peaceful smile. But Lillian wasn't there. He showed up the next Sunday, but she wasn't there. April, May, June, July, August, September, and October passed, and she wasn't there.

After the winter, Stewart came back to look for Lillian every Sunday. Years slipped by. The mallards returned every spring. And the weeping willows wept a little more.

Zach Keali'i Murphy is a Hawaii-born writer with a background in cinema. His stories appear in *Reed Magazine, The Coachella Review, Maudlin House, Raritan, Another Chicago Magazine, Still Point Arts Quarterly*, and more. He has published the chapbooks *Tiny Universes* (Selcouth Station Press) and *If We Keep Moving* (Ghost City Press). He lives with his wonderful wife, Kelly, in St. Paul, Minnesota.

Leaving New Orleans

Krin Van Tatenhove

"This is my favorite part of the drive," said Alberto.

We were cruising over the 18-mile span of the Atchafalaya Basin Bridge, en route from San Antonio to New Orleans, windows open to the swamp's humid aroma. Slanting sunlight of a late summer day dappled its surface.

"*Alguna vez hiciste esto cuando eras niño?*" Alberto asked.

I briefly turned my head to see him moving his hand up and down outside his window, mimicking a bird, a plane, or a spacecraft. My Spanish was still sketchy, but I understood the gist of his question.

"All the time," I answered. "Especially on long and boring family trips."

Alberto chuckled, a feeble sound, far from his usual resounding laughter, and I was struck again by his decline. He was in the final stages of pancreatic cancer, having survived two chemotherapy regimens. At first, his oncologist objected to our road trip, but she relented when she found out the reason.

"This will likely be his last chance to see him," I told my wife, Lisa. "They've been estranged for a decade and Alberto hopes to make amends."

She shook her head, having never understood my relationship with my older Cuban friend. "Well, I hope it works out for both of them. Just be careful."

I had booked an Airbnb near the French Quarter, close to the pulse of Big Easy nightlife, but I doubted we'd be carousing. Alberto's sole objective was to meet with his only child, Arturo, who had been released from Louisiana's Elayn Hunt Correctional Facility to a halfway house in Metairie. Now in his mid-60s, Arturo had done time for multiple DUIs, the final one resulting in a violent crash that thankfully injured no one but himself. He had recently sent a cryptic message to his father. *I want to see you,* it said. *There's something I need to say.* Alberto had written scores of letters to his son over the years, finally giving up hope of a response. When it arrived so close to his death, he grasped at the chance.

"Do you want to cruise by the halfway house and scout it out before we go to our room?" I asked.

"No, *estoy cansado.* Let's just get a meal and turn in early. I want to be ready for tomorrow."

"As you wish."

Alberto took a sip from his glass of beer, another sign of his condition. He usually drained it in a few gulps.

We were seated in the courtyard of Robert's Gumbo Shop, a block from Jackson Square. Locals and tourists packed the tables around us, and a syncopated Zydeco tune filtered in from the street. My friend had been silent during our meal, avoiding eye contact. He had a half-eaten po'boy on his plate while I worked on a bowl of crawfish etouffee, nursing my own drink, not wanting to get more intoxicated than him at this delicate phase of his journey.

As I studied him in the light of the patio's outdoor lamps, I thought of how he had always seemed larger than life: six foot two, well-muscled, his olive complexion showing his mixed French and Spanish ancestry. Now, just past his 81st birthday, his pale skin and sunken chest gave witness to his mortal battle.

I reflected on his uniquely American story. At age 18, he left his family and joined the Cuban Exodus that fled to Miami after Castro's victory. There, he lived on the streets until the Cuban Refugee Center, initiated by the Eisenhower Administration, helped him find a job and resettle in Boston. By the time I met him, he was a journeyman electrician. I was visiting some friends in an apartment building and Alberto's balcony was adjacent to theirs. We struck up a conversation and soon discovered that we shared not only an interest in construction skills, but a love of reading and a quirky sense of humor. I later did some odd jobs with him and our relationship began to grow.

Now, he looked up at me with a weak smile. "You remember when I picked you up at the San Antonio airport that first time?"

I grinned and nodded. "How could I forget?"

He had relocated to Texas, and since my prospects had dwindled in Boston, he enticed me with the promise of work. In those days, the Alamo City's airport was small, and you could drive up next to the debarking planes. When I came down the ramp, I saw his vintage Cadillac parked nearby. He had mounted the horns of a steer to the hood and was dressed in a Stetson hat, jeans, chaps, boots, and a frilled western shirt. He looked like the proverbial rhinestone cowboy.

"Howdy pardner," he had said with a fake Texas accent,

then moved to embrace me as we laughed from our bellies. We then proceeded to a taqueria for enchiladas and margaritas.

"You have to admit," he said, "I nailed it as a *Tejano vaquero*."

He lifted his drink and tilted it towards me. I did the same and we clinked glasses. Then he grew somber again. I waited, knowing he wanted to say something more, but not pushing it, letting his thoughts ripen.

"I keep thinking about those early years," he finally said. "I was such a *pinche* macho asshole. Always pushing Arturo to be a man, never understanding his quiet nature. Louise constantly told me to go lighter on the kid, but I was my usual stubborn self. She told me he cried himself to sleep for months after I left."

Louise, of Irish-American descent, had married Alberto against her parents' wishes. When their relationship fell apart after a decade, Alberto moved back to Miami for a while, but Louise's strict Catholicism kept her from granting him a legal divorce. Arturo was 10 years old when he left.

"I hear you," I said, "but you know as well as I do, you can't go back and relive those choices."

"Yeah, yeah, but the memories won't leave me alone. And all the drinking I did around him? *Jesucristo!* I remember sitting in my recliner and watching football on Sundays. I would point to Arturo, lift my empty bottle and say, 'beer me up, boy.'' What an *hijo de puta* I was."

Alberto had always been hard on himself and others. After I joined him in San Antonio, we shared a remodeling business. He could do the work of two men in a single day, and if we had a crew member who slacked off even slightly, Alberto would give him a tongue lashing. His favorite phrase was, "work hard or you'll end up under the bridge." Personally, I loved his style because it aligned with my own high energy and standards. We kicked ass and made a ton of money.

"I've said this before, amigo," I offered, "and I'll say it again. You can't blame yourself for Arturo's alcoholism. If it hadn't been you, someone else would have offered him his first drink. You either have the disease or you don't. It's a form of Russian Roulette that people across our country are playing every day."

"*Claro, pero* it doesn't make me feel better, no matter how many times you say it."

He pushed his plate away with its half-eaten sandwich and drained the last of his beer. "Let's go back to the room. I want to be as fresh as possible in the morning."

We walked the short distance, Alberto moving slowly and unsteadily, breathing heavily. Then we took turns using the shower. When I came out after mine, he was already asleep on his bed, snoring softly.

I awoke from a vivid dream of lights and laughter on Bourbon Street. Alberto was shaking my shoulder with a vigor I hadn't seen the day before.

"*Levántate, dormilón*," he said. "We've got things to do, places to go."

I roused myself and dressed quickly, noticing the care he had taken with his appearance. He still had a full head of hair, streaked with gray, and he had slicked it back with some sort of gel. He wore a colorful guayabera shirt, dark pants, and a pair of shined shoes. He had neatly trimmed his moustache, but nothing could disguise the pallor of his skin, and his clothes hung a bit limply on his shrinking body.

"Let's go get some java," he said, "Like the last time we were here."

We took the car a few blocks and found a parking spot near Cafe Du Monde. As we sipped our coffee and munched on baguettes dusted in powdered sugar, we watched the first stirrings of activity in Jackson Square. A few vendors were setting up on the sidewalks. A musician was tuning his kora, a man I'd heard before, his sounds forever synonymous with New Orleans in my mind. A homeless man was sprawled on the ground beneath the famous statue of Andrew Jackson tipping his hat, the monument's head streaked with lines of pigeon dung. The air smelled of horse manure from the tourist buggies, mixed with stale beer and cigarettes.

"I dreamed about him," said Alberto.

I knew he meant Arturo. "Tell me about it if you're willing."

He shifted his gaze from Jackson Square to me. "He was a boy and we were holding hands, walking on the sands of Playa Pilar in Cuba. The sun was setting and I felt a sense of peace. But then he let go of my hand and began to run ahead of me, and it suddenly got pitch dark. I was afraid he would get lost. It was my duty to find him but I couldn't see a damn thing."

He placed his hand on his brow, rubbing his forehead.

"It's understandable to feel nervous," I said. "You haven't seen him for so long."

"But why now? After all the letters I sent. And what does he mean by 'there's something I need to say?' Does he want to unload on me one final time? I deserve it but I don't know if could take it."

"Stop borrowing trouble, amigo. Whatever's meant to happen, try to be thankful that you at least get to see him."

He took a deep breath. *"Es la verdad.* If Louise were here, she would say something like 'it's in God's hands.' I never understood that woman's faith."

He checked his watch. *"Vamos.* I want to be early."

We got back in the car and drove to the sober living home in Metairie, about seven miles north. It was in a quiet neighborhood of older houses that needed care but weren't decrepit. I pulled to the curb.

"Do you want me to walk up with you?"

"Do I look like an invalid? Just go and I'll text you when it's time to pick me up."

I put my hand on his shoulder reassuringly, then he exited the car and walked along a set of large paving stones to the front door. He knocked, the door opened, and after a brief discussion with the person who had answered, he went inside.

Since I had some idle time on my hands, I decided to visit the Metairie Cemetery. I had been there years before on a guided tour, amazed at the elaborate tombs and the stories of illustrious New Orleanians buried there.

I parked in the visitor's lot, then wandered for two hours through the manicured grounds, recognizing many of the sites. The Moorish-style tomb commissioned by Confederate General Beauregard for his beloved daughter Laure; the former resting place of Storyville Madam Josie Arlington, with its bronze figure of a woman knocking at its door; the 60-foot spire marking the graves of Daniel and Mary Moriarty, a final "fuck you" to New Orleans' upper-class who never accepted Moriarty's background as a poor Irish immigrant; the Army of Tennessee tribute to fallen Confederate soldiers, its statue of General Albert Sidney Johnston riding high atop.

I sat on a marble bench in front of a beautiful mausoleum featuring stained glass and wrought iron. I didn't know what the cemetery's smoking regulations were, but since no one was around, I lit a cigarette and sat in the quiet sunlight. Billowing clouds sailed overhead, alternately shifting the shadows of the tombs, like the flickering frames of an old movie.

A memory of Alberto came to mind. He had supervised the makeover of an expensive home in San Antonio, and its owner took a liking to him, eventually inviting Alberto to attend his daughter's wedding at a posh country club. Alberto was determined to present himself as not just the hired help, but as a man of distinction. He spent a lot of money to rent two tuxedos—a black one for the ceremony, a white one for the reception—changing in the clubhouse locker room. He sent me pictures from his phone that showed him standing in the midst of other guests, clearly overdressed but obviously proud of himself.

I chuckled, took a drag of my smoke, and felt a gentle breeze caress my cheek. It brought the smell of new-mown grass, a reminder that long after the dead dissolve into soil, nature continues its cycles.

I thought about Alberto and Arturo. Despite the easy affirmations of motivational speakers, I knew firsthand that real second chances are rare. My own father and I had never cleared the air between us. I recalled my grief at his funeral, staring down at his body in the casket, thinking of all the things that needed to be said but never would. The recollection still stung after all these years.

But I also treasured the joyful second chance that had happened in my love life. After the failure of my first marriage and the depression that followed it, I despaired of ever finding another partner. Then I met my soul mate, Lisa, and discovered the miracle of unconditional love and support. I was grateful for her every day.

Maybe everything *is* possible, I thought.

I'm not normally a praying man, but I whispered a few words: *If you're listening, God, look favorably on this father and son reunion.*

My phone chirped in my pocket. I pulled it out and saw a text message from Alberto.

I'm done. Come and get me.

I ground my cigarette underfoot, picked up the butt to

deposit in a trash can, then turned to retrieve my friend.

He was quiet and clearly emotional as we began our return trip. His cheeks quivered as if he was barely holding back his feelings. I noticed a white envelope protruding from the pocket of his shirt. As I had long ago learned with my friend, I stayed silent, letting him decide when or if he wanted to share what had happened.

We had just gotten on the Atchafalaya Basin Bridge going west when he finally spoke.

"Man, I never expected that."

"Expected what?" I asked, noticing with a quick glance that tears were streaming down his pale face.

He swallowed a couple times, trying to collect himself. "I thought he would vent his anger on me. Instead, he asked me to forgive him. Do you hear that? *Me* forgive *him*? *Dios mio*!"

"Forgive him for what?"

"For never taking the time to understand me, even with all my faults. For always blaming me for his mistakes rather than taking personal responsibility. For not seeing that underneath my macho behavior was a man who had always cared for him."

Alberto began to cry softly, a sound that filled the car for a moment. "Then he told me that he loved me."

I was deeply moved, putting my right hand on my friend's shoulder. He reached up his own hand to place it on mine, gently giving me a squeeze. In that touch, I felt all of the bonds we had formed over the years. Then he took that hand and rolled down the passenger window. Once again, the smell of the swamp engulfed us, an odor of verdant life underpinned by decay.

I looked over briefly to see him flying his hand in the air. Up and down, up and down, and then suddenly his arm fell and draped over the windowsill. I knew instinctively what had happened. I knew he was gone. With tears on my cheeks, I drove the final distance to the end of the bridge and found a turnout where I could park.

I got out my phone and called 911 to request an ambulance, then scooted closer to Alberto, feeling for a pulse and finding none. I noticed again the envelope protruding from his pocket. Though it felt like an invasion of privacy, I removed it, opened up the flap, and pulled out a faded Polaroid print. It was Alberto and Arturo when the boy was young, probably just before Alberto moved to Miami. They were standing on the deck of a boat, Boston harbor behind them, holding large fishing poles in their hands and smiling brightly for the camera. At their feet was a string of cod, striped bass, and bluefish, the spoils of their adventure. I flipped the picture over. Scrawled in black ink were the words *A great day together, July 12, 1969.*

I scooted even closer to Alberto, put my arm around him, and tilted his head on my shoulder. Then I waited, the car filled with the whooshing sound of traffic, until I heard a siren in the distance.

I thought again of my Cuban friend in his white tuxedo, his face beaming with pride, recalling a toast he often gave when we shared cervezas.

"*Salud, amor, pesetas y tiempo para disfrutarlos!*"

I held him tighter and said, "Here's to second chances, mi amigo."

Krin Van Tatenhove is a writer, visual artist, and spiritual adventurer. He was a Presbyterian pastor for 34 years, serving in a variety of settings but always an advocate for ministries of justice. He has also been an organizer for Habitat for Humanity, a substance abuse counsellor, a hospice chaplain, an Army Chaplain, and director of a non-profit. His 40 years of professional writing experience have led to countless articles and 17 books. You can freely download most of his work—including art collaborations—by visiting krinvan.com. Krin holds a doctoral degree in ministry from McCormick Theological Seminary. He is married, has four children, and lives with his wife and disabled adult son in San Antonio, Texas.

Stone Castings

E.C. Traganas

Herculaneum, 79 AD

(Back in the 1980s, over three hundred carbonized skeletal remains were discovered submerged along the coastline of Herculaneum, the ancient city that perished during the colossal eruption of Mount Vesuvius in 79 AD. Although most of the victims remain nameless to this day, the excavated ruins have revealed poignant intimations of daily life in a once vibrant and bustling town. 'Stone Castings' endeavors to memorialize the final powerful hours of a young girl and her brother as they struggle to comprehend the collapse of their world.)

She had seen her mother again in her dream early in the morning. It had happened a few times already during the last week. She was reaching out to her with hands outstretched as if in a welcoming gesture to a long-lost daughter. She was dressed in the purest white raiment: a clean, flowing ivory stola girdled at the waist and breast with gold bands inlaid with iridescent jewels. In her mind's ear in the depth of her sleep, she was certain she heard her mother's voice calling out to her, "Justa, Justa! Don't worry, only the good die young..." Was it to reassure her that she had safely made the long journey and had passed into the Underworld and was now in the comforting hands of the gods?

Justa woke, dazed and reflective, and recited her morning prayers at the lararium with unusual solemnity as she poured oil into the lantern and filled the offering bowl with grains of salt: *Purga mentem, purga corpus, purga animum. Be thou well, Mother Vesta, and may your flames guide and protect us. Ita est! — Your will be done.*

There was something strange about the air as she exited the gate with Luca, her little brother, at her side. An acrid, metallic odor seemed to irritate her nostrils like the burnt and carbonized charcoal her father would prepare in a brazier for his drawing sticks. She shrugged it off while Luca skipped ahead, jumping from one stone paver to the next, peering into the empty alleyway lined with clay amphorae and barrels of olives and fermenting fish sauce.

"Will we find him, Justa?" he asked in his small thready voice as he looked up at his sister.

Peculiar things seemed to have occurred during the night, she mused. The neighbor's rooster had been crowing interminably well into the early dawn hours and then went silent altogether as if its larynx had been strangled. The street dogs were howling in chorus like a pack of wolves, responding to each other's barking as if in secret code, and then by dawn Mauro, their housedog, had mysteriously run away.

"He'll be back, Luca. Don't fret," she cooed softly, looking meaningfully into the boy's deep brown eyes, as deep and dark as the rich ashy soil surrounding their own neighboring hilltop of Vesuvio where the ancient gods slept.

Justa reached inside her cloth bag and pulled out a jagged shiny object. Its opalescent surface glinted in the faint morning sunlight. "Keep this stone with you always for good luck," her mother had said, holding it up to her with a trembling hand just before her passage into the Afterlife. "I found this in the rubble of the last great tremor that shook our village years ago, before even you were born. May you never live through dark hours like I have…"

Justa held the stone up to the light and admired its raw, ancient beauty, wondering at the mystery of this fossilized relic that seemed to freeze and compress the flow of time in the palm of her hand for all eternity. In a flash, the gem suddenly lost its luster and faded under the shadow of a cloud that now passed overhead.

It was already past the second hour; the sun had been up for nearly two hours. There was much to be done before tomorrow's Festival of Opalia in honor of the harvest goddess. They had to be off to the fuller's to pick up her newly laundered white tunic. Father will be so proud to see me assisting in the temple proceedings, she beamed to herself.

"Luca!" she called. The boy had disappeared into a corner street and was urinating in a municipal latrine. Soon, she observed, the fuller's slaves would be coming around to empty the troughs and collect the yellowish liquid reeking of ammonia for their washrooms to bleach and whiten the city's linens.

"Look!" Luca cried, pointing up at the sky.

Justa's gaze was transfixed by a massive plume of darkness bulging outwards and ballooning upwards to a staggering, unfathomable height, higher than she thought possible. She felt her neck twisting and craning to comprehend the enormity of the colossal spectacle that was unfolding above them. The umbrella-like cloud was expanding from above the nearby mountain crag and appeared to puff outwards and uncoil itself southwards towards their neighboring city. She thought of their father who was still in Pompeii finishing up his painting commission at a patron's villa.

"Papa should be home by tomorrow," Justa smiled at the boy. "He'll be safe until then."

Inwardly, she wondered why the atmosphere was so eerily silent, why they heard no sounds from the looming mountain crag. If there was any discord within, she hoped the gods would quell any disturbance. At most, she thought, they would be sure to expect a cooling summer rainfall by day's end.

She took Luca by the hand and led him down towards the main avenue and into a side street past the Decumanus Maximus and up a narrow alleyway. "We have to stop by the tutor's house and register you for school, young man. I promised Papa. You will be attending the Ludus like all boys your age. Will you be sure to teach me everything you learn, Luca?"

Her brother was unresponsive and stood frozen in his tracks. Justa had to admit to herself that her stoic charade was not working anymore. Little Luca sensed something was clearly wrong and stifled a howl.

The second story that housed the schoolmaster's domicile was empty. Dense, coal-like darkness was swiftly engulfing them. And now, Justa felt the paving stones lurching ever so slightly underneath her sandals. There was a faint crackling in the air like the gentle flakes of falling snow touching the earth in an early autumn caress. Holding back a rising sense of panic, she raced to retrace her steps with her brother in tow. She could hear a surging commotion in the distance. Looking up, she noticed people clamoring onto their roofs to get a closer look at the billowing black-stained canopy that enveloped their sister city to the south.

Justa lost all track of time in the ensuing mayhem. Hours seemed to scuttle away like the crows that were now flying helter-skelter in every direction. Two, three of the birds dove towards them and then ricocheted back upwards, each unable to gauge height or depth. She felt her heart pounding. Crows were always a bad omen, her mother had said.

The rain of ash flakes intensified until the patter became a drumming noise and the deafening percussive clatter brought a barrage of frothy pumice stones raining down upon their heads. Brother and sister were stopped at the Decumanus as a mule-drawn litter sped in the opposite direction. Justa recognized the stricken face of her father's benefactress.

"Leave the city!" Ermina called from within. "Get out now. Come inside, there's room for you both. I am heading north—" She ducked her head back inside the cart to deflect a falling fusillade of ash. "Here, cover yourself!" she shouted, tossing a heavy bolster through the window.

"We are waiting for Father—" Justa called, but by then the cart had already sped away with maniacal fury.

She thought with a fleeting wave of nostalgia of the rare evenings in the elegant triclinium surrounded by her father's exquisite wall frescoes as she sat entranced at the elderly woman's feet and listened for hours as Ermina deftly plucked at her antique lyre-shaped kithara. Justa remembered how she would fall into a trance-like reverie and merge with the melting tones that seemed to resonate from somewhere deep in the instrument's hollow wooden cavity, carrying her into unseen worlds of magical sound. Come back to us soon, Lady Ermina, she prayed.

There was now pandemonium on the streets. She noticed her neighbors running past with heavy cushions tied to their heads and shoulders to deflect the bombardment of stones. "We are heading towards the Boathouse!" one of them shouted through the din. "It's safe there. There will be ships coming to rescue us!"

A rescue? Justa pondered. Surely it hasn't come to that, has it? A clay roof tile came crashing down near her feet. Why am I in such a fog? she wondered. Had her dream so anesthetized her? The world was collapsing about her on all sides, and she was as deadened and numbed as a lifeless statue.

"Justa, Justa!" mewled her brother, tugging at her skirt. "Let's go, please!" The boy's high-pitched piping jostled her to her senses until she grasped the urgency of the moment. In a burst of energy, she scooped him up and ran madly, joining and blending in with the mass of humanity swelling out over the main thoroughfare towards the coastline while the burgeoning cloud of volcanic detritus unfurled before them like charcoal ink stains on thickened blotting paper.

She found herself running through the open gates of a villa abandoned by its owner in his haste to evacuate the city, past the open sleeping chambers, beyond the backroom kitchens and private bath. In an eastern alcove of the stately residence she found a modest lararium tucked away in a corner where a tiny oil lamp was burning, casting glimmering shadows on a small bronze statuette. *Divine Salus!* Justa rasped breathlessly, *Guide us all to things joyous and fortunate. Ita est!—So be it.*

There was no way now to calculate the hour through the opaque blackness of the murky atmosphere; she guessed it was well past the sixth hour of evenfall, midnight at least, and wondered how they could have traipsed the streets with such aimless confusion. The roof of their lodging had already collapsed from the weight of the avalanche of rocks and there was now no going home.

She dragged the exhausted child down past the Marine Gate and onto the shorefront where people were scurrying about, blindly feeling their way with outstretched hands in the chaos. When they descended onto the shore they spotted the forms of several men and one or two soldiers waving flickering torches at the newcomers. "Get inside!" one of the men yelled at Justa, motioning towards the direction of the caves.

It was pitch black inside the vaulted cavern. Justa could hear muffled coughing and the desperate clearing of parched throats. They were tripping over the forms crowding the dirt floor. One of them, an old woman, was crouched into a hump, hawking up spittle and phlegm. "Gods have mercy upon us!" she was moaning, rocking herself back and forth rhythmically as if the motion would bring some sense of repetitive calm into the impending madness.

Justa clutched her brother's hand and, after inching her way towards a corner of the stone wall, huddled against the cool rock for safety. She felt a strange, bristled wetness on the sole of her foot and then, before they knew what had descended upon them, a familiar sound of snuffled barks was filling their cramped space.

"Mauro!" Luca cried, stroking the muzzle of his beloved pet. If the dog had somehow sensed sanctuary in this remote crypt, then surely we, too, will have a safe haven here, Justa thought trustingly.

The soft whimpering and choked sobs began to die down. Best to preserve one's breath, Justa reasoned. The air— what was left of it—was so brittle and acerbic, like stale, caustic vinegar scorching her throat.

Oh, for a cool draught of fresh spring water! she thought longingly, remembering the balmy evenings the family would spend on the veranda watching the golden sunsets over their city—the very birthplace of mighty Hercules of fabled times— sipping sweetened cherry water and pointing out the skiffs coming and going along the bay.

A profound silence now blanketed the refugees clustered

together in a tight thrashing knot of anguished uncertainty. Outside, a powerful gust of wind extinguished the few torches illuminating the chaotic scene. The hailstorm of rocks suddenly ceased, augmenting an ominous stillness like the rush of dead air into a sealed vacuum.

Far out into the distant waters, Justa felt a wave of unearthly sound rushing towards the beach at what seemed like an unimaginable speed. The walls were now becoming warmer, progressively hotter to the touch. She pulled away, reached into the fold of her pouch to cradle her mother's keepsake gemstone, and hoped wistfully for daybreak.

Author of the critically applauded debut novel Twelfth House, **E.C. Traganas** has published in *The San Antonio Review, Ibbetson Street Press, The Penwood Review, Agape Review, Ancient Paths, The Chamber Magazine, Dark Winter Literary,* and numerous other journals. Hailed as 'an artfully created masterpiece' and a 'must-read', her new work of short poetry, *Shaded Pergola,* was recently released by Tropaeum Press and features her original illustrations. A resident of New York City, Ms. Traganas enjoys a varied career as a Juilliard-trained concert pianist and composer, activities that have earned her accolades from the international press. Find her at www. elenitraganas.com.

Swan Song

Robert Kibble

Becca stood by the edge of the bridge, the oppressive heat of the day finally giving in to a light breeze that chilled her bare arms. The sun hadn't done her headache any good, but nothing did any more. Normally she'd have spent such a stifling day indoors somewhere, but she no longer had anywhere to go. Pubs cost money and they noticed if you tried to nurse a pint all afternoon. University halls were closed for the summer. The library was shut on a Monday, and besides, it would have closed at five. And as for the place she'd once referred to as home…

She looked into the water below, surely still cold, swirling around the brickwork of the bridge, little eddies forming behind each of the wooden poles to guide boat traffic through. She was ready.

She placed her hands slowly on the railing, preparing herself, steadying herself. This was the answer. She hadn't felt so calm in months. The phone in her back pocket buzzed once again. Wouldn't be Mum, obviously—she wouldn't even notice for days. Wouldn't be that bitch of a conniving bastard shit of an ex-lover trying to make things better, saying she was sorry that things had worked out this way and how they should find a way to be friends and that she would always love Becca but...

That wasn't going to be her last thought. Not that cow. No. Peaceful thoughts.

Becca glanced along the river, seeing one late-night dog-walker off in the distance, the whole place otherwise abandoned. She put a foot on the bottom railing.

And something smacked her in the face, knocking her backwards.

A bloody swan.

A stupid bloody enormous swan, right in her face.

She rolled over to see what had happened to the idiotic creature, only to see, instead, a woman, sitting on the bench where Becca had spent the afternoon.

"Good evening," said the woman in a melodic, otherworldly voice. Becca stared at her smooth skin, her thin cotton dress, her long pale neck, and most especially her flowing pale-yellow hair. Indisputably a woman who had been blessed.

"Where did you come from?"

"Just dropped by to see if you're OK." The woman smiled, narrowing her eyes a fraction, giving her what Becca had to admit was an almost-painfully-attractive mischievous expression. She shook her head. This was no time to get distracted.

"I'm not. Now, if you'll leave me alone."

"Oh, don't worry. There's time to fall from the bridge later. First, ice cream!"

The woman stood up, her long light dress wafting around her. Becca couldn't work out what colour it was, as if it was changing as the woman moved. Becca stared at it as the woman reached down to grab Becca's hand. Becca pulled away.

"Oh, I am sorry," said the woman. "How rude of me. I haven't introduced myself. My name's Susan."

"Becca," replied Becca, without thinking.

"So glad to meet you," said Susan, reaching out the hand again, this time grabbing Becca's and pulling her to her feet. "Now, ice cream."

Becca pulled back, but not hard enough to prevent being led off to the steps down to the riverside, and along to where the ice cream stall had been doing a roaring trade all day.

"It's shut," said Becca.

"Not for us." Susan, keeping hold of Becca, knocked on the window. "George. It's me. Midnight ice cream is required."

A rattle came from behind the door, which opened to show an old man, somewhat disheveled as if he'd been woken up.

"You don't sleep here, do you?" asked Becca.

The old man looked Becca up and down. "Not normally, no. It's hard to get comfy in this heat, even on the river." Turning to Susan, he asked, "Two ice creams?"

"Please. With flakes. I love flakes." She glanced at Becca.

The man disappeared inside and returned, two ice creams in hand. Susan took them both, finally releasing Becca's hand, and handed one to her. "Thanks, George."

She turned away and walked down to the riverside, along to the little pier where the riverboats plied their trade to and from the racecourse during the day. She sat down on the edge, her feet dangling almost to the water.

"Come on," said Susan, patting the pier beside her.

Becca stared at her. She could have left the ice cream and gone back to the bridge. But she didn't. She obediently sat down next to Susan and licked the ice cream. It reminded her of her dad. They'd come down here when she was a girl, always having an ice cream, always sitting and chattering about whatever was troubling her. What Becca wouldn't give to have him back, but he abandoned them, like everyone else did, and went off to Australia with another woman, leaving Becca in that house with a woman who couldn't even begin to accept Becca for who she was.

Becca stared at the ice cream, no longer tasting its sweetness, but instead tasting nothing but the cold. She felt her eyes welling up, as they had so often done in the previous weeks. A drop of ice cream ran down her finger, leaving a sticky trail, and dripped down into the water below. A tear, unseen in the darkness, joined it.

Becca found an arm round her shoulders, and for a second felt comforted, before releasing herself and jumping up. "What are you doing?"

Susan remained seated. "Giving you what you need. No more, no less." She licked her ice cream again, as her dress once again seemed to change, this time to a deeper colour, almost a blue, or perhaps that was somehow a reflection of the dark water on it.

"Look, thanks for the ice cream and everything, but I've got to go."

"No."

"No what?"

"You don't have to go. You don't even want to go. Stay a little. Talk. Tell me what's wrong."

"Why? Why should I talk to you? You're a weird woman who dropped in on me from nowhere and won't leave me alone."

"Dropped in." Susan turned a little, and Becca could see she was smiling. "Yes. I suppose I did. Come on, sit back down. You're making the place look untidy."

"Why should I?"

"Because you want to talk."

"No. I don't."

"Yes. You do. You find it painful. I know that. I can feel that bursting inside you, but you have to talk. And I can listen. And then, if you really want, we'll go and jump off the bridge together."

"You're making no sense."

"And you are? All I'm asking is to hear your problems. You've got a lot to work through. I can see that. But if you'd just trust me, you can work through it."

"How would you know? With your beautiful hair and your long neck and wherever you come from and how god-awfully-pretty and perfect you are, you wouldn't know." Becca felt certain of this. The woman sitting on the pier in front of her couldn't have suffered. Not and keep such a gut-wrenchingly perfect face.

Susan looked out to the water, at some swans floating by. "Swans mate for life, you know."

"What?"

"No ifs, no buts. Life."

"What's that got to do with suffering?"

"I lost my partner a few months ago. We'd argued, as we often did, about something trivial. Something pointless and irrelevant and I wish more than anything else that I could go back and change my last words to him. I told him to get lost. Or words to that effect. And he did. He got tangled in some fishing wire round his neck. Stupid fishing twine, left behind by ignorant people who don't realize how dangerous littering into rivers can be. He couldn't cry out, couldn't change or he'd have strangled himself, couldn't free himself. If I'd been there he'd have lived. But I'm a stupid selfish creature who wasn't there for him. Not a day goes by without me regretting that final day."

Susan swiveled round on the pier so that she could look

155

up into Becca's face. "We were supposed to be together forever. And now he's gone. And I cry when it hits me, but I live in the moments when it doesn't. And right now, there's something more important to do. Which is to get you to tell me what's wrong."

Becca stared, and then sat down again, realizing she still had her ice cream in her hand. She licked it again. Her hand was sticky with the amount that had melted and run down to her wrist.

Susan shuffled back so they were both facing the water again.

"My girlfriend left me."

Susan nodded but said nothing. Becca had begun. This time she would continue.

"My dad swanned off to Australia with another woman."

Susan waited.

"My mum hates me and hates who I am and who I want to be and who I love even if on this occasion she did turn out to be a conniving backstabbing cow, although that's not Mum's responsibility, but she hates everything about me, probably because I remind her of Dad, and she hates even mentioning Dad."

Susan finished her ice cream and leaned back on her elbows, slightly behind Becca.

"I can't concentrate on studying anymore because everything else is so messed up that I'm going to be kicked out of Uni. I get headaches all the bloody time which the doctor tells me are psychosomatic and wants to send me to a stupid psychiatrist about."

Susan said nothing. Becca looked down at her legs, dangling over the side, and wondered if the dress had changed color again. It was definitely silvery now. Maybe it was the moonlight.

"All my friends sided with bitchface, so I can't speak to any of them anymore."

Susan leaned forward, and again the arm gently reached round Becca's shoulders.

Becca looked out into the blackness. "I can't go home. I don't have any friends. I don't have anywhere to go. All I've felt is pain for as long as I can remember, and there's no point. I don't want to carry on. I don't want to try. Everywhere I go I'm going to be reminded what a total failure I've been, what a total failure I am." She felt her face. Tears. "And now I bet I look awful with my mascara running, right?"

Susan looked into her eyes and smiled, then laughed.

"What's so funny?"

Susan put a hand to Becca's cheek and wiped away some tears. "It is true. Your mascara has run dreadfully."

Becca stared. "I've told you what's wrong, and all you comment on is my makeup?"

Susan put her second hand on Becca's other cheek and held her. "You do not look awful, Becca Cavendish."

Becca recoiled. "I didn't tell you my surname."

"Oh, you must have."

She pulled back and stood up. "I didn't. I definitely didn't."

Susan lifted herself up on her hands enough that she could get her legs under her, then gracefully rose.

"Look, I don't want your sympathy. I don't want anything. I want to feel numb."

"You want to feel happy. And I can make you feel happy."

"What, drug me out of existence like the doctors wanted to?"

"No. Way better."

"Or pretend that you could love this messed-up wreck,

157

so I begin to hope and then you snatch it away like everyone else has? Look, I don't care. I'm going."

Becca walked away, feeling Susan following, but not looking round. It hurt. All she felt was hurt. All she felt was the list of things she'd failed at, and she wasn't going to lose control of this, the final thing she was not going to fail at. For once she was going to follow through with something she'd set for herself. For once she was going to be in control. She took the steps two at a time and returned to the center of the bridge. This time she didn't pause at the railings, but scrambled up, standing on the top railing for a second, until she realized Susan was standing next to her.

"What are you doing?" asked Becca.

"Falling. With you."

"I'm doing this."

"Oh, I know." Susan smiled again, and for an instant Becca's determination cracked, and the possibility, the longing she felt, cut through her. It was too much to hope again. The failure would hurt even more, and she couldn't bear it. She leaned forward and fell.

It all happened so fast from there. She expected cold, but instead a warm hand touched hers, and she saw Susan, still smiling, falling beside her, and then the hands were gone, and instead she felt the wind around her, bursts of cool air wafting up from below as her wings beat above the water.

Becca couldn't breathe, but not because of drowning. Instead she was drowning in experience, in odd movements, in how her body was so light, so delicate, so perfect, responding instinctively to every tiny intention, and right beside her, sleek and as perfect as perfect could be, another swan, flying, seeing, experiencing the same. She felt herself submerged in the feeling, unable to comprehend, simply being, simply existing.

At the bend in the river the two of them, in unison,

lowered their feet and skidded along the water to a stop. The other swan curled its neck round hers, and she couldn't help but respond, the two gently caressing each other.

Becca followed as the other swan paddled until they reached a collapsed section of bank, where they waddled up for a few steps. And then, before her again was the beauty of Susan. Becca looked down at her own black jeans and vest.

She did not have a headache. She did not feel sad. She did not feel anything but elation from the breeze on her skin, the dampness of the ground, the beauty of the night sky with its clear moon, and with the attraction of this divine woman in front of her, turned slightly away, staring over the water, smiling softly.

"What just happened?" asked Becca.

Susan leaned forward and kissed Becca on the lips. "I don't entirely know, but if you've got a lifetime, we could try to find out."

Robert Kibble's work has in appeared in *Writers' Forum Magazine* and EveryDayFiction.com. He won the Nottingham Writers' Club New Writer Competition in 2015 and has had three pieces published in anthologies (*After the Happily Ever-After* by Transmundane Press, *WoW Anthology* by the Exeter Writers competition, and the *Brighton Flash Fiction Anthology*, Grindstone Literary, Pilgrimage Press). He came in second in the Writing Magazine's Epistolary Competition in 2018 and won a monthly Reedsy's Writing Prompts competition. He lives west of London with his wife, a teenage son, and a cornucopia of half-finished writing projects.

Killing Malice
John F. Miglio

My stepmother's name was Alice but I called her Malice because she haunted my childhood and was the evilest person I ever knew—and for years I dreamed of killing her. I didn't always feel this way about her. In fact, when I first met her at the age of eight I liked her right away. Of course I was at a very vulnerable point in my life at that time. I was still grieving the death of my mother, who had died two years earlier from cancer, and I was mad at the world, especially God. How could any kind of merciful God give my mother cancer when she was so young and then kill her slowly and painfully? It didn't make any sense.

It didn't make any sense to my sister Annie, either. She was three years younger than I when my mother died, too young to understand the concept of death and point fingers at the Almighty as I did, but old enough to know that the primary loving force in her life was gone. My father, a dentist and World War II veteran who everyone called the Doc, was also still in a state of grief, but he did the best he could to care for us after our mother's death. The problem was that he had a dental practice to run and was dependent on a series of incompetent housekeepers to fulfill the role of our mother, which was not really part of their job description. After two years of juggling his dental practice while raising two kids without a wife, he was burned out and desperate, and Annie and I were starved for affection and in need of nurturing and guidance.

Enter Malice. The Doc first met her when a patient of his introduced them. Malice was in her late thirties at the time, the same age as my father, and she had never been married, which should have been a gigantic red flag to the Doc, especially in those post-World War II years when most women got married in their late teens or early twenties. The story she gave my father was that she had been in love with a married man for years who kept promising he was going to leave his wife and marry her but never did. A common story for women of that era, but whether it was true or not is open to question.

On paper they seemed like an ideal match. Both of them were attractive and intelligent and of the same religion, Catholic, although neither one was very devout. But perhaps the most important thing was the Doc needed someone to take care of his kids, and Malice claimed she really wanted kids but couldn't have them due to a medical problem, which she never really explained to anyone's satisfaction. What followed was a whirlwind romance, and six months later they got married. It was a large church wedding with many attendees and it took place in a middle class suburb of Philadelphia, which is where my sister and I grew up.

During the run-up to the marriage, and for the first couple of years after, Malice went out of her way to be gracious and charming and helpful to my sister and me, and we got along with her swimmingly. She even flirted with me a little, making googly eyes and telling me how handsome I was. And if something happened that created disharmony while she was playing with Annie and me, she would go into her pocketbook and take out this bag of chewy green candy shaped like small tree leaves and give us each one, saying, "Here's a sweet pill! Let's all be nice to each other!" Beyond that, Malice tried to be the perfect mate for my father, always making him feel special and important, bragging to her friends what "a catch" he was. So, to a young kid, she and the Doc seemed to be in love. Whenever I heard the latch on their bedroom door lock at night, I knew they were up to something of a sexual nature, although at my tender age I had only a vague idea of what it was.

There were also other signs that the Doc and Malice were in love. After my stepmother moved into our house, my father bought new furniture for many of the rooms and redecorated them according to Malice's specifications. Malice wanted our living room to be "a showcase" no matter how impractical it was, and so she got the Doc—who couldn't care less about interior design—to shell out a tidy sum for a marble coffee table with a white Louis XIV sofa and chairs entombed in clear plastic covers. The plastic covers made the furniture very uncomfortable to sit on, but it kept the white seat cushions under the covers immaculately clean so whenever we had company, our friends or family would "oooh" and "aaah" and marvel at how our living room looked "like a museum."

After Malice was done redecorating the house and putting her imprimatur on all the blandishments, she talked my father into removing any pictures of my mother that were in my room and my sister's room so that she could feel less like an outlier and more like our "real mother." To complete the picture perfect bourgeois setting and show his love and affection for Malice, the Doc bought her a mink stole as well as an automatic dishwasher and a console color TV. These were the new status symbols and all the rage in the Eisenhower/Kennedy era when men smoked unfiltered Camels and had three-martini lunches and women went to PTA meetings and gossiped on the phone for hours with friends and family members. All well and good. But then things began to change—and rather quickly, too.

The first incident I recall that portended future problems seemed fairly inconsequential. Malice had made us steak with homemade French fries and salad for dinner. It was a family favorite and the Doc and Annie and I would always compliment her on it. On this particular evening, however, my father didn't say anything, and when Malice asked him how he liked the steak, he simply replied, "It needs a little salt."

Granted, it wasn't a very tactful thing to say, but my stepmother's reaction was not only unexpected but quite disproportionate to the Doc's response. "Oh, I see," she said, standing up from the table, "nothing's ever good enough for you, is it?" She looked at him with venomous eyes. "I try my best to be a good wife and mother and this is the thanks I get? But you know why?" She was screaming now. "Because you don't really love me! You never did! I'm just a glorified housekeeper to you. To all of you!" She paused for a moment, then burst into tears and stormed out of the kitchen.

My father and Annie and I just sat there, transfixed, and didn't say anything. In a way, I felt sorry for her. Later in the evening I asked my father if he loved Malice. "Not like I did your mother," he told me, "but I do care for her." I wasn't quite old enough or smart enough to realize the implication of this admission of truth, but when I became more mature I understood that Malice and the Doc got married for the wrong reasons. The Doc got his housekeeper and caregiver for his kids, and Malice got the kids she supposedly couldn't have, not to mention a nice home in the suburbs and the status of being a doctor's wife. So it was an equitable exchange between them, but it was based on expediency and mutual benefit rather than love. And now that the truth was out, Malice no longer felt the need to play the role of the kind and compassionate mother and became more comfortable with that of the angry, aggrieved wife. At first, it was my father who took the brunt of her antipathy, resulting in weekly arguments and acrimonious personal attacks. As a result, it wasn't long before the nocturnal sound of the latched bedroom door, which previously I had heard a couple of times a week, became fewer and farther between. And by the time my sister and I were teenagers, there was no sound at all.

During this time, Malice had made a complete Jekyll to Hyde metamorphosis and transferred much of her resentment and hostility toward the Doc to me and Annie. No longer did she even make an attempt to be a loving or fair-minded mother. As far as she was concerned, Annie and I were just miniature versions of our father, and a week didn't go by without her picking a fight with one of us for some imaginary slight that we brought against her. Whenever we tried to defend ourselves, she would not tolerate our "back talk" and would either strike out at us physically or punish us by not allowing us to go outside to play. At this point in my life I had not yet studied psychology, but it didn't take a student of Freud to know this was twisted, aberrant behavior more in tune with a fascist dictator than a loving mother. And it got even worse!

Prior to this time, Malice didn't drink, or to be more precise, we never saw her drink, except at parties. But now she was hitting the booze from the liquor cabinet with regularity. Naturally, she wouldn't admit it. Sometimes she would even water down the scotch or gin and blame it on me when my father asked about the liquor bottles' obvious depletion. It's been my experience that some people get merry when they drink alcohol, some get morose or depressed, and some get downright mean and nasty. As you can probably surmise, Malice fit neatly into the third category. One day, for example, after a few drinks, she didn't like the way I "talked back" to her. I was about 12 at the time, and she took off one of her stack-heeled shoes and tried to hit me on the head with it. I blocked the impact of the shoe with my arm, which caused the heel to fly off and expose the metal pins attached to the shoe's leather sole. Undaunted, she quickly took another swing and hit me on the forehead with the exposed metal pins. The pins dug deeply into my skin and caused immediate bleeding. An inch lower and I would have lost my eyesight.

Later in the day, when my father returned home from work and asked me what happened to my forehead, my stepmother lied and told him that I had hurt myself playing touch football with my friends. By this time, she had already fixed her stack-heeled shoe and sobered up. I told the Doc that she was lying and recounted what really happened. Malice could tell my father took my word over hers, so she stormed out of the house, muttering, "Of course, you're going to take the word of your son over the word of the housekeeper!" Hours passed, and when Malice returned home, she and the Doc had another one of their knock-down drag-out verbal fights, which were becoming more and more of a daily occurrence.

That night after I finished my homework and recounted the events of the day, I sat on my bed and began to cry. My tears quickly turned to rage, however, and I began pounding my fist on the thigh of my right leg directly above the knee. With each blow, I pictured Malice's face absorbing the impact, her cheek bones crunching and her nose flattening as her blood splatted into the air and onto the floor. When I stopped hitting myself, I realized that my anger and hatred of Malice stemmed not only from her despicable actions but also from the injustice of my situation—like God taking my mother when I was six years old. It just wasn't fair! But what could I do about it? Nothing at that point. I had to bide my time, and then I would exact my revenge.

My poor sister didn't escape Malice's wrath either. One night, when my stepmother was supposedly helping Annie with her math homework, she lost her temper and kept calling Annie a "dope" because she didn't understand one of Malice's mathematical explanations. Of course my sister objected to the use of the word dope and told her so; this "back talk" was enough for Malice to lose her temper and slap Annie repeatedly across the face, saying, "You are a dope! You are a dope!" Naturally, Malice did this when my father was at work, and whenever Annie or I would squeal on Malice when my father got home, she would always deny it. And then there would be more verbal target practice between the two of them.

There were many more traumatic incidents I could describe, and by the time I was a senior in high school and Annie was a freshman, our family situation was an absolute horror show, a Grand Guignol of physical and emotional torment. One time, when the Doc and Malice were having one of their quotidian altercations, I remember pleading with them to resolve their differences so we could be a "normal family." But it was futile, and later, when I suggested to Malice that she see a psychiatrist, she went into an absolute frenzy, screaming, "I'm not the crazy one here! I was a happy person until I moved into this family!" In retrospect, my sister and I clearly suffered from child abuse, and had this situation happened today, we would have reported it to a child protective services agency. But in those days it was not an option, and parents could get away with almost anything when it came to controlling and disciplining their children.

By the time I was a senior in college, my father and Malice were pretty much living separate lives and Annie and I stayed away from her as much as possible. It was no secret that all three of us hated Malice and she hated us. One day, when I was discussing our deplorable family situation with my father, I asked him why he hadn't already divorced Malice. Then he told me something shocking. As a prerequisite for their marriage, they worked out a financial arrangement in which my father agreed to include Malice on all his assets, like the house, his insurance policy, stocks and bonds, etc., in exchange for Malice paying off his debts.

"It was very stupid of me," he admitted, "but I agreed to it because I was desperate at the time. After taking time off to care for your mother when she had cancer, my dental practice suffered financially. Also, my medical bills sky rocketed because my insurance didn't cover everything and I went into debt. So making the deal with your stepmother offered me a way out of my financial difficulties. Obviously, I regret it now."

"Obviously," I said bitterly.

"I don't blame you for being mad, but if I divorce her, I lose half of everything. And to make matters worse, if I were to die right now, you kids would be in trouble because she would be in charge of the estate. Fortunately, I've been talking to an attorney friend of mine and he thinks he can finagle something to our advantage. I'm going to meet with him next week and see what he can do."

And then the unthinkable happened!

Two days later my father unexpectedly had a heart attack and died. True to form, Malice became even more vindicative after the Doc's death while Annie and I were in mourning. Now that she was in charge of the estate, she informed us that we were living in "her house" on borrowed time. And if we didn't do exactly what she wanted without any "back talk" we would be out on our asses. The unfairness of the situation made me seethe with quiet rage. And that's when I decided to kill Malice.

I had a very simple plan. It was fall, and in the fall it was my job to remove the air conditioner from the living room window and bring it to the basement for storage for the winter. The air conditioner was quite large and heavy, but I was young and strong and could manage it, albeit with difficulty. The idea was to wait until Malice was in the basement doing laundry. I would remove the air conditioner and bring it to the top of the basement stairs. Then I would call to her for help. When she would get about halfway up the stairs, I would throw the air conditioner on top of her, which would knock her down the stairs with the air conditioner landing on either her chest or face. I assumed the weight and impact of the heavy object would probably kill her, but if it didn't I would have to finish the job.

When I told Annie about my plan, she didn't offer any objections and went all in immediately. "Let's kill the bitch," she said. In a way, it amazed me how both of us had no compunction about killing Malice. In fact, we looked forward to it. So I waited until the ideal situation presented itself and carried out the plan. It worked perfectly—except for one thing. The air conditioner hit Malice in the chest and then rolled onto her face and rested against her nose when she hit the ground. As I had feared, the impact didn't kill her immediately and I had to finish the job. She was still squirming around a little, like a stepped-on cockroach, as I walked down the steps and stood over her. She looked up at me, her eyes filled with a combination of shock and horror.

"Goodbye, Malice," I said as I lifted the air conditioner up to my waist then slammed it down on her face. That seemed to do the trick and knock the remaining life out of her, but I did it once more to make sure she was dead.

When the police investigated her death, they questioned Annie and me at length. But we stuck to our story about how the air conditioner slipped out of my hands when I was carrying it down the stairs and fell on top of Malice, who was assisting me to bring it to the basement. Malice's death was ruled an accident and there were no charges brought against me or Annie. With Malice gone, my sister and I inherited the Doc's estate. We both lived in the house where we grew up for a few more years, then we sold it and went our separate ways.

TEN YEARS LATER

"I read that short story you sent me," Jeannie said to me over the phone.

I was living in LA now and working as an adjunct college professor and freelance writer. Jeannie and I had been going out for almost a year.

"What did you think?"

"You didn't really kill your stepmother, did you?"

"No," I replied, "but I almost did. The only thing that stopped me was that I knew the cops would never believe my story. Everyone in my neighborhood knew my situation and how much I hated Malice. There were even times when I said in front of witnesses that I wanted to kill her. Everything else in the story is pretty much true, though."

"Is your stepmother still alive?"

"No, she died last year. She was living in this crappy little row house in a marginal neighborhood in North Philly. Apparently, she had sold the house I grew up in and burned through most of the money from my father's estate. And when my sister Annie went into Malice's house after her death, she told me it was a complete wreck and there were empty liquor bottles strewn all over the place. Annie also told me that she talked to Malice's next door neighbor who said Malice hardly ever had any visitors and spent most of her time drinking herself into a stupor. So when all is said and done, Malice died alone, unloved, and broke. No wonder she drank herself to death."

"Well, that's karma," Jeannie said.

"Or maybe…" I chuckled. "It's my dish of revenge eaten cold."

"Of course it is," she said and laughed. "The question is, do you still hate her?"

"I do," I replied unequivocally.

"And you haven't forgiven her?"

"No way."

There was a long pause, then Jeannie said, "You know, when you forgive someone it doesn't mean that you condone their actions."

"What does it mean then?"

"It means you're no longer giving that person power over you."

"What power?"

"The power to control your thoughts and ruin your peace of mind."

I didn't say anything. Jeannie was a meditator, a Buddhist, and a very spiritual person. Moreover, she was usually right about this kind of thing.

"Do you understand what I mean?" She prompted me. "The reason to forgive a person is to set yourself free. It's a selfish act, really. It's the only way to get rid of the malice in your own heart."

"Hmmm…" I said. "I'll have to think about that."

ONE YEAR LATER

It takes time to forgive a person. It doesn't happen quickly or dramatically, but it does happen if you decide to make it happen by using meditation (which I did) or some other form of therapy to achieve the result you desire. You begin to think about the hatred you have for the person less and less with each passing day, and then one day it's gone! And you wonder why you let it

171

linger in your mind and torment you for so long. But I suppose everything has to happen in its own time. For me it took about a year for the hatred I had for Malice to dissolve from my consciousness.

Regarding my anger and disappointment with God—the God of my formative years, the white-bearded man in the sky who killed my mother—there was no need to forgive him because he no longer existed as a reality for me. He was replaced by the mystery of the universe and the cosmic consciousness. Nevertheless, there are times when I wonder what my life would have been like had I actually killed Malice. Would I have gotten away with it? Or would I have gotten caught and gone to jail? Who knows? These are the thoughts that stories are made of.

John F. Miglio is a freelance writer and the author of the dystopian thriller *Sunshine Assassins*. His articles have been published in a variety of periodicals, including *Los Angeles Magazine* and *LA Weekly*. His most recent articles have been featured in *Wand'rly, Op/Ed News, Hippocampus Magazine, Truthout, the Democratic Underground, Counterpunch,* and *Cynic*. He has also appeared on Air America Radio and Radio Power Network. His novel *Sunshine Assassins* has been called "a bone-chilling political morality fable," "wickedly entertaining," and "unforgettable."

Thus Spake Alan

David W. Clear

"Insane? I was perfectly sane. I knew that the best place for a genius philosopher to hide out was an asylum. Switzerland, no less. Cool mountain air. Clears the passageways to the higher realms. The rest of the world is insane, or haven't you noticed the news lately?"

I was having my favorite sandwich at Panera when I overheard this man in the corner booth, then noticed he was apparently talking to himself.

"Do you hear this guy?" I asked my girlfriend.

"Yeah," she said, "sad, hmm? I mean, we all talk to ourselves from time to time, but not out loud at Panera."

"Maybe I should ask if he needs help? Maybe he's having an epileptic fit?"

"Maybe he's just drunk. C'mon, we've got to get back to work."

We picked up our trays to drop them off and as I passed,

I looked at him directly in the eyes.

"And what may I answer for you, good sir?"

"I was just wondering if you were okay?"

"Okay? Ach, what charming vernacular passes for speech these days!"

"Alan, c'mon, let's go," Susan said, looking frightened by him.

"Don't be frightened, milady. I'm not one of the criminally insane, you know. They are all in Washington, Moscow, London, Beijing, etc."

"Excuse me," I said, but it seemed you were referring to the philosopher Nietzsche, as in his last years in the asylum in Basel, Switzerland."

He leaned back in his booth, smiling impishly, and said, "Referring? Indeed, I was. Are you a philosopher my good man?"

"Alan, c'mon!" Susan pressed.

Our workplace was just across the street. "Go on ahead, Susan, I'll catch up."

She turned and left.

"She's mad at you now, you know," the man said, "I apologize if I've frightened her. She's frightened for you, not herself. Please sit, my fellow philosopher, allow me to assuage any concerns. Talking out loud to oneself in public is a bad habit I must amend if I am to continue living in this barbaric age."

He shook his head. I couldn't tell if it was weariness, disgust, or sadness. Or all three.

"Are you rehearsing for a play or something? Staying in character, you know?"

"Yes, I'm rehearsing for a play. Let's go with that. A play about Friedrich Nietzsche in 21st century America troubling people on their lunch break in Panera by babbling aloud. Do you think it will be a successful play?"

"I would go see it. I majored in philosophy in college. Nietzsche was one of my favorites. That knowledge is little used now in my job as an insurance claims adjuster."

"So, you did go insane just as he did?"

"No, of course not."

"You're working as an insurance claims adjuster?" he snickered. "You'll be talking out loud to yourself soon enough."

I felt insulted.

He sensed it and quickly reached over the table and poked me gently on the shoulder, smiling as he said, "I'm kidding! Insurance claims adjuster, why not? I would wager there are more women than men in that field, hence your comely lunch acquaintance? Ah, sanity, insanity. Waves come in; they go out. Perhaps you best run along now, lest the authorities catch you talking to me. I'm a wanted man, you know. Oh yes, they frown upon inmates checking themselves out of the asylum on their own personal recognizance. And yet it was surreptitiously and deftly accomplished by my anonymous benefactor who secured reservations, funds and identification papers in order for me to board a flight from Zurich to New York, then take a train to this quaint city of yours, Providence, and ensconce myself in one of your finer hostelries. All arranged in order for me to meet you here now, Alan."

Now I felt a little alarmed as Susan had, that he very well might be dangerous.

Again, he sensed it, and again he said, "Kidding! Or am I?"

"Ok, you're an actor and a stand-up comic?" I said, "this has been enjoyable and interesting but I really do have to get back to work, and…" Just then, flashing lights appeared in the parking lot. The police.

"See what I mean?" he said, calmly. "Yes, you best abscond post haste. May I contact you again once I am out on bail?"

"I'll be having lunch here tomorrow."

"See you then, friend."

I walked briskly across the street, then turned back to see two police officers usher him into their car.

The next day he was there as promised. Susan, when I told her he likely would be, opted to eat lunch at her desk.

He was well into a salad when I sat down with my coffee.

"Just coffee?" he asked

"Trying to lose a few," I said.

"Once you're done reading what I'm going to give you, you may lose your appetite permanently," he said, carefully dabbing any salad residue from his voluminous moustache. Yes, just like the one in pictures of Nietzsche.

"What did they arrest you for?"

"What else? Speaking the truth. Oh, sure, it was cloaked in some cover-up about a fake passport and embezzled funds but they really just want to shut me up. So, we must make haste Alan. I'm sorry, your last name?"

"Whitman."

"No relation I assume?"

"To the poet? Not that I know of."

"We must get together with him some time; I find his gift for language positively enthralling."

"Get together? Okay," I said, more convinced now he was likely a homeless delusional with a 19th century suit of clothes.

"Yes, Friedrich," I said, humoring him, "it would be great to sit down with you and Walt Whitman. Hell, I've always wanted to meet Edgar Allan Poe, too! Let's invite him to the party."

"Ah, poor Edgar. Medication, I told him, just get the right antidepressants! They've worked wonders for me!"

"They did not have antidepressant medication in the 19th century," I said, "but why am I even—"

"I'm talking about when I saw him last week! We were hanging out in New York. I see by your expression your patience wears thin. Let me ask, then, before we part. You, my friend, are a writer as well as a student of philosophy are you not?"

"Well, that would be my dream job but— "

"But you think it would be impossible?"

"A little more possible than talking with Nietzsche at Panera about meeting Walt Whitman and Edgar Allan Poe, but yeah, highly unlikely it would ever pay the bills."

I expected some pep talk about whatever you put your mind to, dream big, etc., but instead he just casually added, "You're probably right. You must be exhausted at the end of the day after processing insurance claims. Serious writing would take more energy than you likely have. But before we go any further, let me pass on this most important bit of advice—don't worry about where the writing will take you. It may be to an insane asylum," and he chuckled and sipped his soda. "The thing is, it, like everything else, will take care of itself."

"How do you mean?"

"You're just a scribe, Mr. Whitman. You may die leaving behind a crazy quilt collection of unfinished stories, journals, poems, etc., which will in all likelihood be tossed into the landfill. Or you may whip your oeuvre into shape and become one of those library shelf attention hogs with title after title by your name. Personally, I prefer the middle ground between those two like what happened to me. I knocked out some good stuff, but a reasonable amount, quality over quantity always, with little fanfare and of course much less money. Oh, and be sure to die before gaining any serious recognition and/or popularity. It definitely adds to the cachet."

"Okay, I expect an old college buddy may show up at

any time now to laugh his head off at having pranked me. So, let's keep playing along a little. How is it you speak English so well? Not even a trace of a German accent."

"Ach, Danke Schoen, I've been trying to lose it for 123 years! Sometimes, though, I wish I had just stayed a simple professor. Just while away my time in and out of the lecture halls, dispensing so much pablum, collecting a safe paycheck. Sort of the equivalent of insurance claim processing, my friend Alan. Einstein and Kafka, they worked in offices, nothing to be ashamed of."

"Please don't tell me you've gotten together with them?"

"Well, not Einstein, I mean not many can get into that club! But Franz and I have shared a pint or two over the decades. He's a likable chap once you get to know him. But I was saying, had I just stayed a professor, I might have met a nice girl from Basel, settled down, maybe a kid or two, and a dog, you know. Let someone else suffer for philosophy and be a major influence upon the 20th century. But what's done is done. Pop quiz. What play?"

"Things without all remedy should be without regard: what's done is done. Macbeth."

"Very good Mr. Whitman! How quickly you were able to look that up on your phone under the table. I will not have one of those infernal contraptions, I must remain off the grid, as it is said."

"But you've been arrested? You have a record, you're in a database now."

"And so, I believe we come at long last to our purpose here together. What's done is only done in one realm. We are never without a remedy. Quantum, string theory, multiverse, etc., so fashionable nowadays, isn't it? And yet I sometimes think it's all just an endless rewriting of the Upanishads for the audience of the day."

"I really don't have time to get into that and Schopenhauer."

He chuckled, "I understand. Neither do I, much as I'd love to. We must proceed to the task at hand. You say I was one of your favorites. Wouldn't it be great then if the one and only Friedrich Nietzsche, incarnated somehow in 2024, had sought out a philosophy student working as an insurance claims adjuster, in order to pass on to him writings which have been hidden for 123 years? The writings I created during my so-called 'insane' period. The writings, dare I say, that might make you, Alan, the pre-eminent philosopher of your day once published. I would keep your day job, however."

And he reached down under the table and plopped a large ancient looking satchel upon it.

"There it is! Everything I wrote from the time of the horse episode to the passing of this body you see before you on August 25, 1900. Read it, even edit it if you feel you are up to the task, and try to have it published. But do so under your own name! I want no credit. That's all I need is to open a new can of Nietzsche expert worms. Nothing against the experts, specific fields of study are innumerable, more power to the lepidopterologists for instance, but I need a rest."

I couldn't help but chuckle, "A rest? You've been dead for 123 years! No, wait, I'm not going to play along anymore. You're witty, charming, and obviously intelligent but—"

"But the only question is, will you accept these papers? It was a big effort to write them, keep them hidden from the asylum attendants, and then after my so-called 'death' in 1900, carry them with me through many countries, continents, hotels both grand and shabby, in a lonely nomadic trek through the 20th century and into the 21st until I found the person who was meant to claim ownership of them."

Greed sprouted suddenly in my mind, briefly overruling

rationality. The lost writings of Nietzsche auctioned at Sotheby's for $5.6 million. Having come into the possession of an insurance claims adjuster in Providence, Rhode Island, after they were passed on to him by an insane street person who may have found them discarded in an abandoned building he'd been sleeping in and...no, stop.

"Ok, sure," I said, thinking now this was no college prank but just some sad old man, well-read and with a penchant for drama, just wanting someone to listen to him. And yes, needing some serious meds.

"Merci beacoup! And now if you'll excuse me, I need to use the restroom."

Moments later the police arrived again. They spotted the satchel on the table in front of me and one demanded, "Where is he?"

"He said he was going to the restroom."

They dashed away and then, when I opened the satchel, there was a thick stack of lined paper, tied with a string, yellowed with age, crumbling to the touch, covered in soot and dust and drink spills and fingerprint smudges, and all totally, completely blank of any writing whatsoever.

David Clear: "I am a New England writer; plainly a hobbyist rather than a professional. I had no formal writing education, but many great writing teachers, from office jobs to heartbroken relationships, and even convenience store clerks. I am retired, and I guess still seeking my great writing whale. My novel *Dreaming at the Speed of Sound* is available on Amazon."

A Story You Wouldn't Believe
Shawn Casselberry

Willie sat on a weeks-old newspaper on the corner of Michigan and Adams, across from the Art Institute in downtown Chicago. It was a high traffic area, with rush hour in the mornings and afternoons, and a steady stream of shoppers along Michigan Avenue and tourists going in and out of the museum. His seniority on the streets, almost 30 years, earned him this prime piece of real estate, and he wasn't going to squander the opportunity. With some creativity and a little luck, Willie knew he could bring in a decent haul.

He placed a large McDonalds cup he found in a trash bin at his feet, and leaned against a light pole.

"Good mornin,' Chicago," he started, as people walked by him from both directions. "Have a blessed day."

His clothes, which were a size too big, were the last pants and shirt in the bin at the shelter where he had been staying. He didn't mind the loose fit, it was when the clothes were too tight that he had a problem.

"Do you know what today is?" he asked to no one in particular.

"What's today?" a curious woman with greying hair responded.

Seeing he had her, he sat back and smiled, "It's my birthday!"

It wasn't his birthday, but one thing he learned early on was that if people thought it was his birthday they were much friendlier, and in turn, more generous. It was his favorite story out of all of them because there was something hardwired in humanity to treat people a little better on their birthdays. Technically, it could have been Willie's birthday, he never knew his actual birthday, because he was abandoned by his mother when he was an infant, and none of his many foster parents had bothered to track the information down.

"Happy birthday..." the woman obliged. She felt around in her pocket for coins, trying to find the least valuable ones.

"You know what I really want for my birthday?" Willie asked.

She braced herself, figuring he was going to want a few dollars from her purse.

"For more kindness in the world."

This was worse than if he had asked for money. The woman, now on the hook, squirmed, trying to monetize kindness.

"Oh, what the hell," she said as she opened her wallet and pulled out a five dollar bill and dropped it in his cup.

"You have made this world a much kinder place. For that I am truly grateful."

"You're welcome. Have a happy birthday!"

After the woman left, Willie put on a cheap pair of sunglasses he found on the train on the way in.

"Can someone tell me the time? Anyone? What time do you have, sir?"

"Who, me?" A man in skinny jeans and a Wilco t-shirt stopped, looked at his Apple watch, then said, "quarter til."

"Quarter til what?"

The man looked at his wrist again. "Ten."

"Is it ten already? I'm gonna be late."

"Late for what?" the young man found himself asking.

"Late for my date with Beyoncé!" Willie laughed, revealing a few missing teeth. "You know what, I'm going to make her wait for me this time."

The young man smiled, then pulled a handful of change out of his pocket and emptied it into the cup.

"Sorry, this is all I got."

"Just remember, smiles don't cost you anything, but they can make a huge difference in someone's day."

"I will, thanks."

Willie stood himself up for the next one. His knees cracked, and his butt was numb from sitting on the unforgiving sidewalk all morning.

"Does anyone want to hear a story you wouldn't believe? Boy, do I have a story to tell. Not any story, mind you. A whopper of a story. You, ma'am, would you like to hear my story? Sir, how about you? Does anyone want to hear a story?"

He went on like this for a few minutes until a tourist couple holding bags from luxury stores on Michigan Avenue took the bait.

"What's your story?" they asked him.

Willie looked the couple up and down, then thought for a moment.

"There was this couple from out of town. Where are you from?"

"Dayton, Ohio."

"What a coincidence! That's where this couple was from. Well, they had a good life, no, they had a great life. They had a house, cars, and kids. Do you have any kids?"

"Yes, two," the woman said.

"This couple had two kids as well. But things weren't as perfect as they let on. Stress from work creeped in. The business and busyness of everyday life took a toll."

Willie could tell his story was landing so he kept going.

"They decided to take a trip to Chicago, to get away, and let loose a little bit. They went shopping and bought a lot of things." Willie looked down at their bags again. "A whole lot of things. But you know what they found after buying all those things?"

"What?" they both answered at the same time.

"They still felt empty. You know why?"

They shook their heads.

"Because it's people that are important, not things. It's human connections with people that brings life the most fulfillment. You know what happened to that couple?"

"No, please tell us," the woman replied with tears welling up in her eyes.

"They learned the lesson. They returned home changed. They paid more attention to people, to their kids, and to each other. And my favorite part of the story is, they lived happily ever after."

The couple exchanged a look, then the man reached into his wallet and pulled out a twenty.

"That story was about us, wasn't it?" he asked.

"I can neither confirm nor deny it," Willie said, with his hands up in the air.

The man put the bill in the cup. "Best $20 I spent all day."

"My man."

The couple walked down the street arm in arm, their shopping bags dangling at their sides.

Willie repeated his stories throughout the day with varying results. Some people gave money and some people gave smiles or ignored him completely. The birthday bit was the most effective, but Willie liked switching things up, otherwise he got bored.

At the end of the day, when the cup was full and Willie's body was sore and achy, he left his spot and made his way back to the shelter.

A police officer Willie knew by name asked him how he did.

"My best day yet," Willie answered, as he always did.

Willie saw a woman sitting on the street with a sign that read, "I'm having a bad day," and a cup, only hers was not even half full.

"When's your birthday, darling?" he asked.

"Willie, you know it ain't until September."

"Well, here's an early birthday present." He pulled out a $5 bill from his cup and put it in hers.

"You're too kind, Willie."

"No such thing."

Willie used a couple dollars to catch the train. A homeless teen was sleeping across two seats. He removed the $20 bill the Dayton couple gave him and slipped it in the boy's pocket.

Willie got off the train and walked four blocks to the street the shelter was on. He heard some footsteps behind him. Willie turned and said, "Does anyone want to hear a story?"

Three men jumped Willie from behind. One hit him with a baseball bat in the back of the head, while the others punched him and kicked him as he lay defenseless on the ground. Willie covered his head with his hands, leaving his ribs exposed. He felt one of his ribs crack.

"Brothers, please stop," was all he could utter. They stopped, grabbed his money and ran off.

Willie laid there for a couple hours without moving. The pain was unbearable. A few cars passed by, but no one stopped, thinking he was strung out on drugs and needing to sleep it off.

Eventually, Willie crawled down the sidewalk to the shelter, his head and hands bleeding badly. The staff helped him inside and bandaged his wounds.

After a few days of bedrest, Willie was back on Michigan and Adams, sitting on an old newspaper with a different fast food cup at his feet.

"Do you know what today is?" he asked the first person that passed by.

"No, what?" a tourist asked.

"It's my birthday."

Shawn Casselberry sees the world through stories. He's written fiction and nonfiction books, including a recent novel *The Hemingway Bible* and *Strange Fire*, a collection of dark fiction stories. This story is from his forthcoming short story collection called *The Image of God*. Additionally, he's the co-founder/editor for Story Sanctum and lives in the Chicagoland area dreaming up new worlds. You can check out more of his writing at: www.shawncasselberry.com.

The Vault

Nico Bechiș

The music leaked through the open door and sank into the carpet. With a slight gesture of the hand, Paula invited her client into the therapy room while she lagged behind just enough to breathe in and exhale deeply.

The client sat on the dark oriental chair while Paula zoomed through the registration form. Emily Brown. Delta St, Los Angeles, CA. No allergies. Back problems. Low blood pressure. No pregnancies. No migraines. Dry, sensitive skin. Body concerns. Poor circulation. Lumbar pains. Massage pressure: deep. How would you like to feel after your treatment? Blank space. Consent and agreement. Scribble. Date. August 12th, 2013.

Emily had beautiful, prominent clavicles that glowed briefly in the light of the candles. Paula kneeled in front of the washing bassinet and asked Emily to soak her feet in the warm water. Was the temperature good?

"Yes," said Emily in a ragged, cluttered voice, then coughed and said, "Yes," again, and the word vibrated for a while before the taiko drums in the speakers drowned it.

Paula scattered dried rose buds into the bassinet, then proceeded to wash Emily's feet. The skin on Emily's shins tightened as if she was suddenly cold, but then she relaxed and exhaled over the little concentrical crests in the water. Paula cleared the soap from Emily's feet, rinsed the spaces between the toes, and dried them with the warm towels she kept on her lap.

In her mind, Paula searched for English words to put Emily at ease, but nothing came to her mouth. She wanted to say that the pain in the body comes from a pain in the soul, but as she touched Emily's skin and felt the soft pulse beating against her palm, she remembered Emily's hoarse, unwelcoming voice, and remained silent. She dried her hands before helping Emily put on the disposable slippers, then prepared to get up. A brief electric current surged through Paula's lower back as she stood, the white towel curled to her chest, the warmth from the washing bassinet dampening her hairline. She smiled blindly in the client's direction, and searched for words to explain, to soothe.

Emily looked troubled and uncomfortable, and Paula invited her to lie face up on the massage table. She gently pulled the towel over Emily, then caressed her through the rough cloth, stopping here and there to apply pressure on the meridians. Emily brought the hem of the towel up to her chin, and Paula smiled at this childish gesture.

There'd been a time when Paula, too, had brought the hem of a rough blanket over her nose to fence away the somber sight of the dormitory, the rusty white bars from the empty beds, the shadows. She'd arrived a day too early to the gymnastic camp in Deva, eager to quickly fulfill her dream and win the golden Olympic medal. Her mother had returned that very day to Bucharest, leaving Paula on the stairs of the dormitory as the car moved away, and her mother's blue sleeve flapped along the line of chestnut trees.

Emily waited with her hands on her womb. Paula rubbed her palms vigorously and placed them over Emily's, then pressed slowly but firmly. A wave of white heat washed over Paula as Emily opened her mouth to let go of the air. With her hands still laced with Emily's, Paula moved back and forth, quicker and quicker, until the movement penetrated the slick membrane that separated the two of them, and, for a while, they moved in unison as if traversed by the same current. The pain came to Paula through her hands, heavy and shapeless and deep, and Paula observed it as it rushed through her bones in search of a place to clog.

The colors of autumn had washed away from Deva almost as soon as Paula's mother left, and the greyness that seemed to be the very substance of the city stretched far into the month of May. Every week, Paula would go to school and to training, and on Saturdays she would speak to her mother on the phone in the secretary's office. Her mother would tell Paula to behave and always try her best because soon Paula would go to the Olympics, and mother would join her there. She'd buy a small photo camera and sit very close to the podium, and when the judges would give Paula ten in a row and the golden medal, her mother would be right there, taking pictures. But until then, Paula had to impress her coach and listen to him because he, and he alone, would take Paula where she wanted to go.

It was easy for Paula to listen to Mr. Carp, because he had a deep, vibrant voice, like a trombone. His words seeped through her pores, and her muscles obeyed him before her mind understood his instructions. Move. Arch. Faster. Bend. Flex. Repeat. Again. And again!

The Zen music in the little massage chamber gave way to the sounds of rain rapping against a tiled roof. Paula began the effleurage movement over the left thigh and the hip, slowing down over the root of the toes, the knees, and the iliac crest, and again Emily's body responded with faint throbs. Our past is embedded in our flesh. In fact, the flesh is our living memory, and sometimes memories hurt.

Paula's body had started to hurt when she was twelve. She was training with Mr. Carp on the new Yurchenko vault, a vault that they hoped she would perform for the next Olympics. It was during one of the take-offs, when she had just left the springboard and had begun to rotate up and backwards, that the pain began. It lasted less than a second, already gone by the time she landed on the sponge, barely a symptom of something not yet manifest. Mr. Carp prescribed her three sessions of physiotherapy followed by massage, every week, and her mother, who couldn't at the moment come down to see her, sent glucose and vitamins and calcium tablets from Bucharest and said it was only natural. Paula was growing; when she'd be fully developed, the pain would stop.

She was sent to the camp's therapist, a man with blind, dirty eyes and limp flesh hung loosely over the bones. He was sitting on the therapy bed, with his eyes closed and his hands laced in his lap when Paula got there. The wall behind him was painted white, but the light that crept through the window spoiled it with grey. There was no furniture in the room, only the sturdy therapy beds with white oilcloth mattresses and a small wheeled table, where the masseur kept the electrotherapy machine and the massage oil that smelled of nothing.

Paula told him she was there for lumbar therapy and did her best to avoid staring at him. His eyelids, red, were shut over the sharp curve of the eyes that looked like gymnastic balls ready to roll out of their sockets when he wasn't careful. The masseur pointed his finger towards a place on the bed, very close to where he was sitting, and told her to lower her trousers and take off her shirt. She did as she was told, careful to keep her back towards both him and the entrance, to protect the sprouts of her breasts.

The first session was awkward. Two sets of small blankets inflicted electrical currents into her skin and her muscles, generating contractions that poked at the ball of pain in her spine. The blind man stood by the bed, looking nowhere.

She tried to channel her thoughts away from the therapy room and the pain, to the national team, Mr. Carp, the sequence of steps leading to the cartwheel in her Yurchenko vault, the pre-flight section when she needed to shift her center upwards, away from the horse, to her mom. But one after the other, the thoughts drifted and finally collapsed into her spine, including the masseur who, in her mind, worked as a buffer between her sixth and seventh vertebrae.

She roamed the room with her eyes, searching for a clock, but the walls were bare, and the murky light was too weak to cast any shadow. The masseur drew a white curtain to isolate her bed, although the room was empty, and there was no one waiting in the corridor. A year might have passed before the physiotherapy machine stopped, and the masseur raised the cuffs of his sleeves to feel for the bottle. A drop of oil fell on the man's tunic, gliding down towards the woolly trousers that bagged around his knees, but he didn't notice and continued to grease his hands. When he finally pressed Paula's lumbar, it seemed that his touch, heavy, warm and reassuring, had a power of its own that had nothing to do with the blind man and wasn't explicitly aimed at Paula but somewhere farther or deeper, as if she wasn't the receiver, but the channel.

When the nature sounds in the speakers were replaced by the drone-like, rhythmic strokes of a piano, Paula asked Emily to turn on her belly while she held the towel between them, like a curtain. She filled her hands with frangipani oil and brushed the skin over Emily's soles, starting from the heel, paying particular attention to the inside of the foot. She began with a gentle twist, then squeezed the feet in her palms and rubbed the arch, and finished by pulling the tips of the toes to align the meridians. The pain that came through her hands traveled upwards, along the tunnels in Paula's arms and clavicles.

She continued to train every day with the others, but soon Mr. Carp moved her from the first place in the line of gymnasts to the middle, behind Lavinia, whose face was red and freckled, and Paula should have been devastated, crying, imploring. Still, at the time, the only thing she could focus on was Mr. Carp's voice, his dusky hard voice spinning inside her like the hands of a gymnast performing on the uneven bars. The more the voice swirled inside her, the more afraid she became that she would lose it, that the coach would see through her, deep to the hideous pain, to the dirt that was spreading all over her body, to the smell of her rotting spine.

Every day, she would run to the physiotherapy sessions while the other gymnasts were doing their homework and watch the shadows folding over the white curtain for longer and longer stretches of time. The masseur was her ally, the only one who understood her situation. His hands, to which her skin and muscles had become so accustomed that it sometimes surprised her to feel her own fingers touching the painful area, his hands found their way to her back without difficulty, as if they had eyes of their own, eyes that could follow where the pain was trailing.

But despite the therapy, Paula was tugged to the end of the line of gymnasts, farther and farther from the Olympic dream, forced to wait sometimes for more than fifteen minutes for her turn to come on the balance beam, while some other girl received Mr. Carp's instructions.

There'd been times, before the pain, when Paula had deliberately missed a beat or a landing, only to make Mr. Carp speak to her. Push the horse! Explode! Speed! On a few occasions, his angular face bent slightly to release the words in her direction, and his sour smell of tobacco became almost palpable at the back of her neck. Once, he even gave her a pat on the arm, but since the pain had erupted, she'd felt ashamed and contagious, afraid to be near him.

She didn't confide to anybody, not even to her mother, how bad the pain really was, and every Saturday, in the secretary's office, she listened. The list of clothes that mother had bought for Paula, the number of days until she would receive the passport with the American visa, the presents they'd have to bring back, the sandwiches to be prepared for the journey. But deep, under the words, Paula's mom was begging to be emigrated, to be freed of the iron curtain. This also was to remain a secret.

Her conversations with the masseur were limited. She knocked on the door and said her name, and he laughed and told her to undress and lay on the table. He had asked for a new physiotherapy machine, stronger and more effective, with a single, thicker blanket that covered all of her lumbar region and part of her buttocks. While she removed her T-shirt and lowered her pants, he set the timer on and warmed his palms. And, for a long while, the crick-crick-crick of the timer and their breathing were the only sounds.

"The pain never leaves the body," the masseur said, "you must learn to use it." Then, he searched with his fingers for the nodules of pain, first over the shoulder blades and the back of the neck, then lower, into the lumbar region. He kneaded and pressed and encircled her muscles until his breath became raspy, and his sweat trickled from his forehead onto his hair and his eyelids and down onto Paula's back. And then he moved down to her buttocks and her thighs, and the saliva in Paula's mouth thickened.

She continued to work on the knot in Emily's back, forcing her mind to penetrate the skin barrier, traveling deeper and deeper into the epidermis, looking for blood, trying to pump as much oxygen to the area as the capillaries would bring her, urging Emily's flesh to warm and help with the healing. The pain thronged down Paula's erector muscles.

Sundays had usually been the grimmest because on Sundays, Paula got to see Mr. Carp only once and even then, just briefly, in his office. On Sundays, the training was conducted by Mr. Florea, Mr. Carp's second, and Mr. Carp sat at his desk with the thick yellow folder waiting in front of him. The pen, green with a golden ring in the middle, sat next to the folder while Paula took her seat. Mr. Carp asked for Paula's name, just for the record, and wrote the date, 12 February 1984. Four months before the Olympics. He used small, precise letters that glinted for a second, and Mr. Carp waited for them to dry before he asked for the parents' names and occupations, although he knew perfectly well that Paula had only her mother. Secretary.

"Counter-revolutionary activities?"

Paula shook her head.

"Anything suspicious the Party should be informed about?"

Paula shook her head again, but this time, Mr. Carp didn't look at her, and Paula had to say in a loud, clear voice, "No, nothing to declare."

Then Mr. Carp's pen scratched the paper, insisting twice or three times on the "no" while Paula held the door for Lavinia to enter.

She pressed her knuckles against Emily's back. The flesh was soft and welcoming, apart from the nodule where the pain resided. She felt her own muscles tightening at her back, where the pain had reached the lumbar region, a sharp and familiar cut.

She had awoken at some point during the night, with a disgusting, rotten taste brought by the pain. The lights were off, but a strange, eerie light drifted in the room as if pushed back and forth by the breaths of her roommates. It must have snowed after she went to sleep because the air was stiff and crumbly, and a new uneasiness filled Paula's chest. She pushed herself to the edge of the bed and further into the choppy air of the dormitory, propelled forward not by her legs but by the strange sensation stirring inside her. The lights were off in the corridor, and the air was fueled by a frozen breeze that scrunched at her skin. She walked to the window at the end of the hall in a trance, intrigued by both the breath of the snow and the response in her body, with the pain leaking through her knees. She stopped for a moment to put her head down and press the tips of her fingers onto her eyelids, the way she'd seen the blind man.

Something creaked at her left, and Paula saw Mr. Carp's head tilting in the space between the door and the wall. She opened her mouth, but there was no sound she could produce.

She knew she needed to explain, justify herself, hint at the snow that had led her astray, but her mouth remained mute.

"Sleep," Mr. Carp said, hunching his back as if he was trying to protect something hung on his chest.

Paula nodded but didn't move, her eyes still hurting as she took in the stripes on Mr. Carp's pajamas, seeking an excuse.

"Spine?" Mr. Carp asked, and she nodded, grateful to both Mr. Carp and the spine, and Mr. Carp said, "Come," and, after a pause, he said "ointment," and Paula felt the pain at her back throbbing, as if Mr. Carp had just awakened it.

Mr. Carp's bedroom had very little furniture, only the bed, a ragged wardrobe with one of the doors slightly unhinged, a chair, diplomas and pictures of a younger Mr. Carp, and a brown velvet curtain. The ointment tube lay on the bedside table next to a glass-painted lamp, in the shape of a fish. The fish had its mouth open as if gasping for air, and the light that came out of it made a yellowish circle onto the wall. Paula's stomach gave a faint rumble.

She was curious but also ashamed to be there, to be disturbing the fragile air with her putrid breath. Mr. Carp pointed his finger to the bed, then to her blouse, but she hesitated, the pain might be infectious. Mr. Carp opened the lid and squeezed the tube. With her gaze glued to the circle of light on the wall, she lifted her blouse, trying to muffle the sound of her inhales. Mr. Carp's hands were warm but scratchy, like her own hands, chipped by talcum powder. The unease in her chest traveled to the spine, shifting back and forth in the rhythm of Mr. Carp's palms. With each movement, Mr. Carp's fingers uncovered new patches of her body, scratched a new vertebra, a rib, a fragment of the shoulder blade. Part of her wanted him to stop immediately, afraid that the masseur would discover the scratches, but something pinned her down, waiting, craving for

Mr. Carp to lubricate her, not just the back but also her face, her head and her eyes. It was hard to keep her breath quiet, and the air became heavy with the sounds of her and Mr. Carp's exhales. Back and forth, back and forth, with the pain goring deep inside her.

Emily was panting and moaning under Paula's hands, her body responding automatically to Paula's touches, arching and bending unnaturally in an attempt to increase the span of their contact. Paula herself was afraid to let go, and she continued to work for a long while, longer than necessary, and the pain at her back continued to throb, sending vibrations that washed over Paula, Emily, the therapy table, and the walls, swelling with each inhale and contracting with each exhale, like frost and thaw in the rivers, like a mother's hand waving steadily before the curtains are drawn.

Mr. Carp hadn't reached out to her until after Bill Clinton visited Romania, after the fall of the communists. It was the height of the summer, and Paula recognized his voice immediately, the familiar cadence broken by the distance and the static, saying he was sorry for her loss.

'Thank you,' she said, and stared at the lights that travelled the darkness on her wall with the speed of the passing cars. Suddenly the distance that separated Paula from her mother's death solidified. Destitution, prison, lung cancer. The pain at Paula's back stirred, gathering strength from the warmth of the bed, pulsing.

So many miles away from her, Mr. Carp breathed, and the words tumbled out of his mouth and into Paula's ear. 'I thought you'd come back after the Revolution," he said, and she left her head drop onto the pillow and felt reassured, almost glad of the distance that separated them.

The soft chime in the speakers meant that the massage session was coming to an end, and Paula's mind drifted towards the tasks waiting at home. Scrub the bathroom, cook dinner, apply ointment. She slid her palms over Emily's back, one last scanning for dangerous lumps of pain, then covered Emily with the towel. The air travelled upwards from Emily's skin, as if her entire body, not just her lungs, had let out a deep exhale that was shoved into Paula's nostrils. The frangipani oil smelled different on Emily, more rarefied, almost salty, as if it had been mixed with the air above the sea, with a sense of freedom. Paula held her breath, trying as best she could to avoid it and almost blurted out loud that it's all an illusion, we're never free. With rapid movements, she tidied the folds of the towel, and travelled her hands from the lumbar to the first cervical vertebra, to the heels, for one last stretch. Finally, she lifted her palms and brought her hands into prayer, and diverted her thoughts to the pain locked at her back.

In the year that followed Mr. Carp's first phone call, the Romanian Olympic Committee flew him to LA and Mr. Carp invited her for dinner. They ate at the hotel's restaurant on a curved sofa upholstered with grey, artificial leather, and Mr. Carp ordered a burger with fries and a beer. The years since she'd last seen him had amassed weight to his muscles and bones and sanded the lines on his face. They ate in silence, with their knives and forks, as if their hands were still covered in talcum that might poison the food. Beads of sweat had formed by the edge of Mr. Carp's hair. She watched him wrestling with the burger, drawing his index finger every twenty seconds to push the golden rimmed glasses back to the root of his nose, smiling uncomfortably whenever he looked at her. In person, he was less talkative than on the telephone, and Paula asked whether he planned to visit Vegas for a day or two after the conference.

"Don't like gambling," said Mr. Carp not looking at Paula but at the psychedelic wall behind her and then to the left, at the greying window. "Gambled only once in '84, when I put you on the Olympic team, and almost got my chest burned," he added and the words remained hanging between them, like the tiny beads in his beer glass that gathered in a foam at the top.

To hide the sudden flush in her cheeks, she asked him if he wanted any dessert but he declined and produced a box with rum chocolates wrapped in the Romanian flag. They asked for the bill, and Paula paid and they got in a taxi and there was a moment of silence after the driver asked where to, but then Mr. Carp said "Home!" and Paula didn't say anything. Only her spine arched on the backseat of the car as she struggled to recite her address.

She waited in the corridor for Emily to put on her bathrobe, gather her things and leave. There was little oxygen left in the room, with a strange, stale smell to it, and Paula pulled the curtains aside to open the window. It was a large window, as large as the wall, leading straight into the spa's back garden where the last of the afternoon sun was glowing onto the palm trees, the yellow poppies and the grass. Later she would have to stop by the shop to buy bleach and carrots and beer for Mr. Carp, and maybe a bottle of wine for herself.

She gathered the towels from the massage bed and dusted the mattress. The leather was still warm, and Paula looked down at her hands covered in a thin layer of oil that smelled like Emily. It seemed hard to believe that Paula had once used those same hands to haul herself over the horse in an Olympic championship. She poked her fingers into the therapy bed to test its resistance, expecting, against her better judgement, to feel her skin choppy and dry from the talcum. She looked back and went to the door and opened it, and the corridor poured into the room like a dark runway. She took off her slippers and socks and measured the carpet with her bunion feet. When she had reached the twenty-five meters, she drew a line with her toes, arched her spine and lifted her left arm, with the fingers spread like a fan, a gesture that had been distinctive for her generation of gymnasts.

In the distance, the light drenched the therapy bed in white and gold, making the oily handprint shiver, blinding her. As she was thrusting her arms upwards to prepare for the cartwheel, the bulk of her pain freed itself from the lumbar and drifted between the shoulder blades and farther, to the base of her skull, then spread down to her heels and her toes. But she was already pivoting.

Nico Bechiş is a Romanian writer living in London together with her husband and two children. Her stories gravitate around the narratives ascribed to women in South-Eastern European societies, strategies for solace, and the impact of totalitarianism on literature. She is currently working on a novel about prostitution, parenthood, and modern slavery.

Best Land Plans

Thomas M. McDade

I paid a goodbye visit to Windburn Barn figuring a bunch of
college kids would have rented it by now, but there were no
cars in the parking spots. I stuck my hands in my jean pockets
thinking that would make me look like an off-the-beaten-path
stroller and not a thief or arsonist. Moving closer, I saw that
the door was slightly ajar. I pushed with my foot. The hinges
yawned. I heard a rhythmic creaking that sometimes lulled me
to sleep during Heidi's drug recovery. I remembered Freshman
English, landscaping, and how happy she was leaving for Texas
to ride thoroughbred racehorses. That armless rocker I'd logged
so many miles on was facing the sad bay window and occupied.
I cleared my throat. The chair scrunched around. A Zippo
flamed. Despite boy-short hair and swollen face, I recognized
Heidi. It was a ghostly scene, ear studs sparkling like attendant
fireflies. She'd suffered a black eye. The way she wore her hair
sometimes to class would have hidden it. She'd told me the

Zippo was a good luck charm, belonged to her grandfather.

"Heidi, what happened? What are you doing here?"

"Just a coincidence," she said frantically like someone trying to pull an excuse from the air. "The hay truck I hid in to escape stopped down the street. I'm like the scarecrow. I need brains, too." I recalled Spence had a t-shirt with a flatbed trailer image but I couldn't picture the cargo.

She pulled a piece of hay from behind an ear, stuck it in her mouth and lit it like a cigarette, before dropping it on the floor to quickly burn out. She wore what must have been jockey boots.

"Do you remember Carolyn singing?" she asked.

"Yes, especially 'Scarlet Ribbons,'" I hummed. There was also the sorrowful "Green Fields." I reasoned adding that one would not be welcome.

"I sang it to myself over and over while in the straw, my baby in a manger. I thought of rolls in the hay and the grief they've caused me."

"Carolyn disappeared and so did Spence."

"They were a mysterious couple, nympho and druggie but good roommates and employers." I wondered how a couple often pleading poverty came up with the money for a nearly new dump truck for one thing. Carolyn never mentioned a sugar daddy.

"I hope no harm came to them. I wonder if they still do landscaping." The name of their company was Best Land Plans.

"Remember scattering hay for new lawns?" Heidi asked.

"Yes, the grackles watching and waiting for the seed." Why would hay be hauled from Texas to Denver? Maybe she hitched first and that was her last ride. I'd leave it at that. I was starting to feel like a DA. Was hay the same as straw?

"You've bounced back before."

"I'm helpless, broken."

"I'm leaving town," I said. "My car isn't much but more comfortable than your last ride. Come with me. We'll go to Seattle, wave to the people leaving on cruises like in the Thousand Clowns movie. It's a trek, all right. From there we could catch a ferry to Alaska, get work on the Pipeline."

"May we sort of return to some reality for a moment, Tom?"

"I know that line but it was 'Murray.'"

"Webb beat me up after I told him I was pregnant. When I was unconscious, he cut off my hair. I burned down his barn. Nothing alive in it, just tack, oats, hay and the dope he used on horses. He won't involve me. I know too much. The greedy bastard will be happy with the insurance money. I thought about igniting this place, too. Eliminate another chunk of my past. I dream faces, laughing and smirking, our class, gamblers who'd curse at you because they'd bet the horse that tossed you. So what if you broke a leg or your spine. High school yearbook pages and movie mug shots haunt me, but not you."

"Your nightmares were just fate biding time to get to now."

"I like that," she said. "This is all I own, Tom, except for my top shelf boots and the ratty, smelly clothes I'm wearing." The chambray shirt with a ripped pocket reminded me of Navy issue. She flicked the Zippo, moved it around for me to see and she was right. I lightly kissed her lips and face. Her breath was fresh. Maybe a tube of toothpaste left behind in one of the bathrooms or a Life Saver in my room, case closed.

"Heidi, I think we should send the Zippo white water rafting in Boulder Creek. It's run out of luck and could be used as evidence. Let's scram, find a place to eat. After a couple of hundred miles we'll get a room and rest up for our journey."

"Good thinking," she said, "but not the Pithy Pines

Motel type." She nearly laughed, which must have hurt. She'd lived there before Windburn.

"Never," I said with conviction.

I considered bringing the rocker with us but I had no rope to tie it down on top of the Plymouth. What a ridiculous idea anyway. I made a quick trip to the car and back. I gave her my hooded sweatshirt and had another thought.

"Wait a minute. You must be dehydrated. I've got a six-pack of Sprite sodas in a cooler." I brought back two and she chugged them and they were colder than I thought. She hugged herself and said "brrr" a few times.

I rescued her from falls twice walking to the car. Her damaged face stood out more in the daylight. When I got her into the passenger seat, I ran back to shut the barn door. Before I started the car, she pulled up the hoodie and shirt sleeves to show her tattoo: "Nothing good gets away." The "good" was bruised yellow. John Steinbeck's initials were under it. She'd talked to me about a literary tattoo wish while taking a break from planting a Japanese garden. She reached over and squeezed my thigh.

"The 'good' is you, Tom."

"I say you."

Sweatshirt hood snug on her head, she said in an elderly voice. "I'm Sister Mary Heidi."

"Bless us and save us!"

At Boulder Creek she side-armed the Zippo like a major league pitcher. I helped her take off her jockey boots. "Best way this," she said, stripping to her bra and panties. She nearly toppled. There were more bruises on her legs and back. I got a half-used bar of Irish Spring, an unclean towel, jeans, socks and a flannel shirt from my seabag. She did her laundry, including her underwear. She stood in shallow water and gave herself a good soaping. I saw no sign of pregnancy and I wasn't about to ask. She did look a bit with child while we were walking out of the Windburn and she was hugging herself. She dove, stood on her hands. As she emerged, I looked at the ground. A passing kayak nearly tipped.

"Look at me, Tom. I'm yours for the taking." Her breasts were unscathed and firm, nipples as dark as raisins and the size of some super capsules Spence had in his drug arsenal he kept in a toolbox along with a wad of paper money. He'd offered me a sample high but I chickened out. She slowly put on my clothes. I ran back to the car for a belt. No way that my jeans would work. She rolled up the shirtsleeves. She tugged her jockey boots on.

"Ever ride a horse, Tom?"

"Does a merry-go-round count?"

"Nope, we've got to get your feet in irons sometime, galloping beside me." Thoughts of shackles and chains while being led to court swept over me.

"How about just putting a donkey under me? I'm a Democrat." This was Lourdes all right. She put a foot on her knee and joined her hands over her head.

"Hee-haw," she yelled through a hearty laugh. She wrapped her clothes in the towel and put them on the backseat floor. On the road again, we were silent five minutes or so. I timed it by the dashboard clock. Heidi kick-started us. "I feel great Tom. That was a baptism."

"Miraculous and Amen," I said.

"Are you sure you want to go through with this? Nothing's ever been easy for me. I don't want to jinx you."

"We'll take it easy and easier," I said. I felt my words were awkward and escaped by suggesting that she open the glove compartment and take out the paper folded in half, my poem that I thought was the best I'd ever written. She read it aloud, slowly. I didn't tell that it was about an aquarium in a one night stand named Madeline's apartment.

Utility

The fish an inch at best
Wear stripes of neon blue
Running gill to fin
As if in league with eels
Promoting electricity
Darting household tanks
As though famed embers
From a storybook blaze
They spark in and out
Of ceramic castles
Like dreamy arsonists
As guppies blessed
With spectrum tails
Loll and wave in
Flimsy praise like
Squads of second
String cheerleaders

"Perfect, I love it." She kissed me on the cheek. "Arson, arson everywhere and a trout likely ate my Zippo." I felt guilty that it wasn't a poem about our landscaping days.

"The idea came from a short Faulkner story from class about burning down barns." Carolyn told me she hoped to be a college football cheerleader someday.

"You sure can link things, Tom." Then she exclaimed, "That truck ride cost me my baby."

"I'm sorry."

"You don't have to be."

"I want to be, honestly." Just the bottom word of her tattoo was showing, "Away." A big shame on me for letting, "awry" slip into my mind. She pulled my shirt out of my jeans and shot her hand up to my heart.

"I believe," she said. She took a nipple, rubbed it between two fingers for a moment like one might a lucky charm or a combination knob on a safe. She made a cross with a finger before exiting. "I'm gonna make your heart shake, Tom." I recalled Carolyn's stolen line, "You backlight my dreams."

"Do it in a gentle, gentle, way." Was Carolyn her romance consultant?

"Of course, I'm going to poem you."

The car ran beautifully, just one loud blowout. I almost swerved into a guardrail.

"I thought we were being shot at," said Heidi. When we got out, she squatted to look at the expired tire. "Yup, flat as a pancake," she said, her face in a parody of a grin. She'd described herself that way when she caught me looking down her shirt when she was pushing a wheelbarrow full of gravel. Before she stood up, I ran my hand across her breasts.

"You got a memory on you," she remarked. I fetched the spare, scissor jack, and four-way out of the trunk. Heidi stood back, hands on hips. We took turns with the wrench but no lug budged. Were they welded on? Finally, I had to hold the wrench level and Heidi stood on an end. The creaking was like a horror movie door—on a barn. The spare had some nice threads. We stopped at a K-Mart to buy Heidi some new clothes.

"I'll pay you back, Tom."

"You already have," I said. She picked up a pink travel bag and dropped in make-up for her eye, three colorful blouses, a skirt and a pair of black jeans and some black stockings, negligee, flimsy bra and garter belt, two bandanas, and $3.99 pearl ear studs. The sexy stuff surprised me but what male would argue? Heidi acted like the finery was run of the mill.

"I need a break from the silver. You might be calling me

lettuce ears when these toys turn mossy," she warned.

"I like bunny better," I said. My mother gave me a defective pearl tie tack from a costume jewelry factory where she worked for a year. I straightened the crooked pin with pliers. What would she think of Heidi?

"Ha, I'm a centerfold!"

"Of the year," I said. She spun her eyes. In the parking lot of the Double Suds, she skillfully fashioned the red bandana so that it covered her head, secured it in the back. She disguised her eye perfectly but none of the red marks on her face.

"I got tossed out of the convent."

"Welcome home."

I filled a couple of pillow cases. I took a pair of clean jeans and a t-shirt. Heidi carried in the new black jeans and blouse. I wore a pair of PF Flyers, Heidi my shower shoes. We wanted to be complete, down to our socks. Heidi asked if I was sure I locked my side of the car. "I wouldn't want to lose my jockey boots."

"What a dummy I am! I wore those work boots landscaping, full of valuable us memories." I hustled back to check. I had not.

There was a unisex restroom. We took turns and exited wearing what we'd carried in, fatter pillowcases. While we were quizzing each other from a Reader's Digest "Word Power" section, a couple of kids approached. The girl was maybe five or six. She had Carolyn's blonde hair. Her dress was a blue polka dot.

"I'm Jane, this is my brother Mark." He wore of all things a fireman's helmet that was too big so I couldn't see if he was fair-haired like Spence. Those two characters lingered in a corner of my mind as if I'd done them wrong. Mark did carry a very small dump truck. His khaki pants were high waters.

"We're pleased to meet you," said Heidi. "This fellow's

Tom."

"Did a bunch of bees sting your face?" asked Jane. Mark made buzzing sounds.

"That's exactly what happened," said Heidi. "You are very smart. Maybe you'll be a doctor."

"I'd fix your face in a jiffy. I do have a toy kit, stethoscope and all."

"I want to be a fireman," said Mark. Jane tapped on his helmet.

"You guys ever hear of Winnie the Pooh?" asked Heidi.

"Not yet," said Jane.

"Here you go." Heidi closed her eyes and recited as if she were holding the book. The story featured a bee hive. She was great. I thought she'd break up thinking of her lost child she'd never read that tale to.

The woman who'd been folding clothes was finished. She came over. "I hope they were no bother."

"They were a delight," said Heidi. Jane and Mark waved goodbyes all the way to the door.

"Someday I'll entertain our own like that," said Heidi.

I nodded and touched her "bee stings" with the back of my fingers. An old lady read the riot act to her husband. She held up a dollar bill she'd found in the clothes she'd just taken out of the washer.

"Literal money laundering," said Heidi, smiling.

"Efficacious," I said taking up where we'd left off on the quiz.

We had lasagna at Joe's Venetian. Heidi loved the pepperoncini in the salad. At her request I over-tipped the waitress whose shoes were in bad shape. She spoke broken English. There was a black ribbon pinned to her uniform next to her name tag that read Philomena. Heidi wondered if she'd lost a child and hugged her. As we left the parking lot, a '49 or

'50 Ford sped by. Its paint was grey primer. There were flames painted on the front door and the hood.

"Like a bat out of hell," I observed.

"Like us, Tom." We passed barns with Mail Pouch Tobacco advertising painted on them.

"Did you ever chew or is it chaw?" asked Heidi.

"The second one is best. No, but guys on the Ramply who worked in places you couldn't smoke did. They spit the overflow into Dixie Cups. There was this one guy. No, it's too gross to tell." "

"Was each cup poured into one and a crazy sailor downed it on a bet?"

"Yes, indeed."

"Yes, gross is the word. Did any of them throw their Zippos into the ocean?"

"More likely they were gifts to night ladies."

"Tips for tits," she said, giggling and cupping hers.

At the Road Crest Motel, Heidi waited outside while I took in our gear. She insisted I carry her over the threshold. What would she have said or done if I'd divulged I'd done the same with Carolyn at the Pithy? She insisted we shower alone but we toweled each other off. She put on her K-Mart lingerie.

"Do I look cheap, Tom?"

"You know I'm thinking of the tired old 'million dollar' response."

"That's not green and wrinkled, is it?"

"It's fresh government issue. Hell, let's leave it at spectacular!"

She bent forward, palm up, then dropping it slowly. I took my English Leather from my seabag and pointed out the saddle.

"Wow, I never noticed that before," she said. We scented each other, as she called it. She slowly stripped like an exotic dancer. Heidi matched Carolyn's cheerleading themed eroticism with her racehorse riding moves. When she'd tuckered me out, she got out of bed.

"Here I am at Boulder Creek," she said.

"Ah yes!" She called her stance a yoga tree. Falling back into bed, her opened arms welcomed me. Raised up on my elbows, she locked me in her eyes and read a poem off the top of her head. I'd never seen her write anything down.

Charm Tom

Naked I stood
On my hands
In the creek
Where the lighter
I'd hurled after
You swore
Its lucky charm
Duty was done.
But no not so
Bolt upright
It lurked on
A fire red rock
And as I reached
A trout saw.
I was kin
All my bruises aping
Her prism scales
Gobbled it up
Like a glitzy lure.
And flashed off
Leaping once
Out of

The kayak
Rippled waters
Breathless
I yearned
To land
Under you

"I said I'd poem you."
Damned if I didn't get tearful.
"Close your eyes," she said. She licked them. She said that a literary review containing the poems she'd write about this night would be housed in plain brown wrappers to confound the censors.

I went out for grub early the next morning. Before going into Coffee Plus, I fiddled with the radio. I found a rusty screwdriver and pliers in the trunk. I managed to remove the unit from the dashboard. Two tubes were loose. All back in place, I hit the radio face with the heel of my hand a few times but nothing interrupted the static. It wouldn't turn off.

"What's going on here?" asked a cop wearing mirror sunglasses.

"I'm trying to get the damn radio working."

"They're tricky," he said. I showed him my license and registration and that was it.

"Enjoy the finest scenery in the nation, young man," he said after tapping the hood for some reason. I bought a couple of cheese and egg sandwiches, large coffees, and cheese Danishes. The waitress had fingernails polished the color of coffee with a shot of cream. She gave me a card and punched out two cups, eight more and a freebee.

I kept checking the rearview mirror to make sure the cop wasn't tailing me. I had a hunch Heidi would require mucho explaining. Check out time was ten. We took our time eating while watching an episode of Bewitched. We showered together and made love. I took our bags to the car. Heidi was standing inside.

"How about lugging me over the threshold again for good luck?"

***

I hit a bump in Idaho and it fixed the radio. A news show reported an unsolved bank robbery. Boulder truckers were protesting road conditions. A 67-year-old trucker died of a heart attack after a pothole hit knocked bales of hay off his truck and he tried to put them back.

Heidi covered her mouth and chin with a palm before digging both hands into the hoodie pouch. "That radio's lying but doesn't know any better."

"Okay, but we'll probably hear it again, can't turn the radio off or change the station. It would be dangerous to put my fingers in my ears."

"I have to be honest with you, Tom."

"Whatever you've done is water over the Hoover and under the Tappan Zee."

"We'll see. While I was hitchhiking I saw the hay truck parked at a rest stop. I climbed on and found a gap between bales. I don't know if it was a pothole or a deer in the middle of the road, but he slammed on the brakes and nearly went off the road. I was thrown off with the three bales that cushioned and saved me. He got out of the truck cussing away. I was sitting up. 'A scare-boy gift,' he shouted. He grabbed for my crotch. I got up and ran into the woods. He followed until he collapsed. Tom, he thought I was a boy!"

She punched the palm of her left palm and gritted her teeth. The static stopped. "I'm half-sorry the vermin died, but he would have raped me or killed me after he found out I was a woman. I think he scared the baby out of me. It happened in the woods with the planet Venus and a piece of moon as witnesses."

"You've failed again to run me off. You're all woman. I sure know that. That trucker's number was probably due to come up soon. Someday you'll write poems about that night and become famous. I'm saying I'm sorry for the last time."

"There's one more verse, Tom. Earlier, the truck pulled into a closed gas station where a car was waiting. There was an exchange. After the trucker death, I had enough wits to check his cab. I found the package under the seat that contained three inches of hundred dollar bills. I managed to secure it under the hoodie when you were going back and forth from the barn to the car and hide it for us."

"You are a rascal! What would Pooh do?" I asked thinking of the dripping Laundromat buck.

"Tom, Spence gave the driver the money. Carolyn was sitting on the hood of the car."

"Best Laid Plans, by landscaping smugglers." I said.

"There you go connecting again and here's my plan. We've got to stick with the ink. We've got to do a lot of good with the cash."

We bought a VW van at Five Star Phil's Hardly Used. Phil's eyes tried to leave his head when he saw the bills. We took the van to The Mechanic Maven to get any lemon seeds removed. He'd just finished hanging a "Going Out Of Business" sign. The bent mechanic was a sad looking fellow but perked up when Heidi flashed some green. He turbo smiled and straightened up like a marine at attention. He explained all the repairs in detail. We gave him three hundred. A hundred over the two he'd quoted.

As we were leaving, he took down the defeated sign. We distributed money in church poor boxes and gave them to people running shelters and soup kitchens. If there were nuns, Heidi asked if they knew of a Sister Mary Heidi. There was never a match.

"Sister Mary Unique," she'd joke when leaving. We ended up at Wyoming Downs. Heidi was back in the saddle. I was learning the business from the ground up, mucking stalls. Heidi's first Wyoming winner was a filly named Zip Away.

Thomas M. McDade resides in Fredericksburg, VA. He is a graduate of Fairfield University. McDade is twice a U.S. Navy Veteran serving ashore at the Fleet Anti-Air Warfare Training Center, Dam Neck Virginia Beach, VA and aboard the USS Mullinnix (DD-944) and USS Miller (DE / FF-1091).

Polyps

Matias Travieso-Diaz

1

My knees and hands were bleeding and hurt like the dickens, but I was still holding onto the seashell I had picked up from the darkened area under the beach house. My older cousin Toto, who had accidentally pushed me down onto the sharp stones, lifted me up by the armpits and set me straight. His head almost touched the house floor overhead, but he carefully drew me out of the confined space into the sunlight.

"I'm sorry" he apologized, noticing the battered condition of my body.

I opened my eyes with a start. It had been a nightmare, a vivid recounting of an event from my childhood, seventy years before. Only a dream, but it had left me shivering with cold sweat. Then, as I became fully awake, the dream turned into a full memory.

There had been a wild storm the night before, and I had

sought refuge in my parents' bedroom as the thunder boomed and lightning flashed, seemingly just outside our door. Yet, cradled in my mother's comforting arms, I went back to sleep as quickly as only a seven-year-old can.

The morning showed bright and clear. The tempest had blown itself away, leaving only a roiling sea in its wake. Toto and I put on our swimming trunks and ran out, streaming across the short sliver of sand that passed for a beach and splashing into the water. The surf was cold and it was hard for me to keep standing against the back-and-forth rolling of the waves. I still had not learned how to swim and could only waddle. We tried horse-playing, but soon gave up as we kept bumping clumsily into each other.

"This is no good. Let's get out and go looking for shells," urged Toto, who was eight years my senior and therefore the leader in our activities. We shuddered the cold water off our swimming trunks and started walking up and down the beach searching for treasure. It was a disappointment: the beach was littered with all manner of sea shells, but thanks to the violence of the storm they were mostly broken, and the few that remained intact were small and uninteresting.

"Tori, let's go back home and have some pancakes," Toto suggested, and I dutifully followed him.

We reached the large beach house across the road from where we stayed. We had been cautioned to stay away from that property, for the owners were nasty and their huge guard dog was nastier still. We were skirting around the house when Toto grabbed me by the arm. "Tori, look!" he called out, pointing at something under the house.

As all beach houses near the ocean, our neighbors' home sat on wooden stilts that protected the property from flooding. The area framed by the stilts was dark and extended the length and width of the house, and I normally stayed clear of it, since I found it a little scary. But Toto was directing my attention at the pebble-covered surface under the stilts.

I looked. The sea had washed under the stilts during the storm and, in retreating, had left behind a few sea shells that seemed in better condition than the ones on the beach.

We walked over to the back of the house and looked behind the stilts. Toto had focused his attention on a narrow area that was hit by the mid-morning sun. There, a number of shells gleamed on the light among the paving pebbles. "One or two look fine!" he shouted excitedly.

I ran ahead of him and squeezed behind the stilts. There were, indeed, several shells that seemed to have survived being tossed and crashed around. Taking a close look at them, though, I realized that those that were intact were small and drab. I was getting ready to come out when I saw something glinting in an area way back, near a metal utility box. It was tantalizingly near, but almost out of reach. I got on my hands and knees and started crawling towards the object. Toto, who was following closely behind me, bumped into my back, lost his balance, and crashed on top of me, sending me sprawling against the pebbles.

I tried to get up, and in the process my hands, naked feet and knees got painfully scraped by the sharp ground stones. Ignoring the pain, I stretched my right arm forward and plucked the object from the underside of the box, where it had become wedged.

As Toto got me out of the darkness and I was able to examine the loot, I gasped. It was a shell, almost as large as my hand. It was irregularly shaped: pointed at both ends, with a fat cavity on the bottom where its snail inhabitant used to reside. Mostly white, it had a series of delicate butterscotch strands of coloration running diagonally around the shell's surface, which was covered with spine-like protuberances. (I later learned that shells of that type belong to the *murex* family, and the larger ones are prized by collectors.)

I was admiring my acquisition when Toto brought me back to reality. "We need to go home so you can get your cuts and scratches treated. Let's go!"

* * *

My mother was normally placid and easygoing; for that reason, her reaction as I came into the house, followed by a sheepish Toto, was remarkable. She pressed me to her bosom, crying dramatically: "My baby! What happened to you?!" As I stumbled for words to explain our adventure, her mood became increasingly angry: "What were you doing under that house? Didn't we warn you those people were bastards?! Didn't I tell you to stay away from them?! What if they had sicked their dog on you?! And look at what you have done to yourself!!" And then, turning to Toto, she vented some of her anger on him: "And weren't you supposed to look after Toribio? Wait until I tell your mother!"

Toto started to explain: "We were just looking for seashells…"

"Looking for seashells? That's stupid! He's just a little boy but you're old enough to grow a beard! Get out of my sight!" Toto made a hasty departure, and made himself scarce the rest of the day.

My mother took me to the bathroom and proceeded to clean my wounds, applied mercurochrome to disinfect them, and covered a couple with plastic bandages. She ignored my wincing but, as she was working on one of my knees, noticed that I was still holding the murex shell in my right hand. "And what's that?" she asked sharply.

I cowered. "Just a shell I picked up."

"Hand it over!" she demanded.

I reluctantly gave her my prize. "Is that why you got under the neighbor's house?!" She was getting upset again.

"Yes, but..."

She finished bandaging and let go of me, but not of the shell.

"Well, the punishment for your disobedience is that I'm going to get rid of this shell!" She waved the murex in front of my eyes.

"Please, no...!"

She got up and returned to her bedroom, still clutching the seashell. I was left behind, disconsolate and humiliated.

2

As I grew into my teenage years, my attraction for the sea did not wane, but intensified. This was perhaps tied in an obscure manner to the memory of the marine treasure that I had once lost to my mother's fury; in any case, I welcomed every opportunity to go to the beach. However, I no longer searched for seashells and ignored those the tide cast my way.

When I was fourteen, my father took us to a marine park for a short vacation. There, I went snorkeling for the first time and found myself swimming by a shore coral reef. It was a life-changing revelation. I marveled at the rounded underwater hills that seemed planted on the seabed; their scalloped surfaces, like giant brains, were hosts to myriad tiny fish, sponges and mollusks of all kinds. The hills were crowned by fantastical protuberances, tubes, wide lacy fans, antlers, bunches of berry-like little spheres... And the colors! Through the clear waters of the bay, I delighted in the deep reds, oranges, yellows, blues and purples of the convoluted walls of the coral hills, which seemed to join together into walls that stretched forever, hugging the coastline.

I was hooked. From that day forward, my ambition was to get to know the secrets of those coral forests. I went to college and majored in marine biology, and soon learned that those enticing corals were not plants but animals, and harbored secret lives even more exciting than the busy goings-on on their surfaces. For the architects of these underwater forests were humble beings known as polyps: small, transparent little tubes with sac-like bodies and mouths encircled by tentacles. They are soft, nocturnal beings that protect themselves from predators by constructing strong external skeletons made of limestone. Their bodies harbor tiny algae (which give the corals their beautiful colors) and the spaces between adjacent corals serve as shelters for many small creatures that find protection there from would-be predators.

I became a college professor and a marine biology researcher. Investigations of life in the coral reef informed my research and resulted in a spate of papers that gained me international recognition in life science circles. The last paper before my retirement was perhaps the most famous. Entitled *"Polyps and Men – Life Lessons from the Coral Reef,"* it was a semi-philosophical work whose main thesis was presented upfront in the introduction:

> As I studied the life cycle of coral reefs, it dawned on me that it is an imperfect, but powerful analogy to the fate of human beings. The life of a polyp is brief, but the strong skeleton it builds joins the myriad other shells built by its predecessors, contemporaries, and successors, to form a community that continues to grow year by year and endures for many centuries. An individual polyp may be gone, most likely forgotten altogether, but its contribution to the species lasts as long as the species itself continues to thrive. And thus, a modest but essential path to immortality is granted to each individual regardless of whether its short existence was filled with joy or sorrow;

whether its deeds were celebrated or condemned by its contemporaries; whether it lived in isolation or provided shelter and comfort to others.

The paper elicited much commentary and was debated well beyond marine biology circles. After my retirement, I was invited to travel to Miami to present it on the occasion of my receiving a lifetime achievement award by the American Society of Underwater Biology. I am in my late seventies and do not travel much, but could not pass up the opportunity to give one last speech on my favorite topic.

The talk was a success, as far as those things go, and I was assembling my papers and getting ready to leave when I received an unexpected visit. A young man in his twenties, with a large cardboard box held precariously under one arm, approached the podium.

"Hi. You may not know me, but I'm Carlos, the oldest son of your nephew Gerardo."

I was taken aback. My late brother and I never got along and had hardly spoken in the last five years of his life. I also was out of touch with my nephew, who had stayed back in Miami while I went to Hawaii to attend college and, later, to teach and study the vast coral reefs in the Hawaiian Island chain. Because of the long distance that separated us and the strained family circumstances, I had never seen Carlos before.

"Oh. I'm happy to meet you, Carlos. Thanks for coming." I felt a little embarrassed for not trying to contact Gerardo and his family in advance of my trip to Florida.

"You are welcome. It was a very interesting talk."

"Thank you. How are Gerardo and your mother?"

"Mom is fine. Dad could not come because he was in an accident at work and the doctors have ordered him to stay home."

"An accident? What happened?"

"He fell off a ladder while doing a home inspection. He is fine, just has a broken leg that needs to be mended before he can move around."

"My plane does not leave until four tomorrow. I can come visit with him tomorrow morning."

"That'll be great. He always talks about you." There was a pause. Then he continued: "Anyways, he sent me here to deliver this box to you."

"What's in it?"

"When great-grandmother died, your brother went through her possessions and put in this box some items that belonged to you. I imagine he was intending to give them to you some day, but the two of you never got together, so my father inherited the box and the assignment to deliver it to you. And now he handed it to me."

"I see. Thanks a lot." We brought the box to the speakers' table. It was taped, but the tape was old and brittle and was easy to remove. When we lifted the lid, there was a smell of old and decaying paper.

I quickly rummaged through the contents. Old diplomas, photos from my school days, a few medals I had collected over the years, a couple of books, a diary I had started keeping as a freshman in college and abandoned almost immediately. Then, on the bottom, a large irregular object.

"What is that?" asked Carlos.

At first, I could not reply, since a knot had developed in my throat and was choking me. Finally, I muttered: "It's a shell I picked up once when I was a kid. I haven't seen it in many years." I could not go on, as my eyes filled with uncontrollable tears.

3

That night, at the hotel, I could not sleep at all. Memories and regrets circled around my head like birds of prey hunting for a victim. I sat at the desk, lounged on the easy chair, and tossed around in bed. The result was the same, too many questions with no easy resolution.

I had managed to toss away those whose behavior had caused me pain or not met my needs or expectations. Staring at the seashell I realized how much my mother had loved me and how little affection I had bestowed on her after that fateful day seventy years ago. I was never cruel to her, or outwardly inattentive, but in my heart of hearts I had erected a barrier that had prevented me from giving her a full measure of love. I recalled how people had remarked about my composure the day of her funeral, when I failed to shed a tear as she was taken away.

My marriage had been another instance of failed love. Almost from the start I recognized that my wife and I had little in common and shared few interests. Instead of seeking to accommodate her infatuation with soap operas and sales at Bloomingdale's, I retreated into myself and buried myself in work in order not to have to seek common grounds with her. When she died ten years ago, my mourning was brief and insincere. I never realized how much I missed her and how important a part of me had been peeled away with her passing.

The rest of my family could well deserve to be discounted, but I wrote them off too easily. My brother was a failed human being, but I never tried to meet him halfway. It may not have mattered, but I never gave myself a chance to find out. And the rest of the family, my nephew Gerardo, my other nephew Agustín who had left for Spain never to return, they all were innocent bystanders deserving more attention than the holiday cards and presents I sent every Christmas.

And the tally extended as well to my friends and acquaintances, from days old and new, whom I had let go casually by allowing our friendship to wilt for lack of care like a plant abandoned on a window sill.

The sad truth was that the attention that I had bestowed on my profession had been denied to other parts of my life. I was, sadly, alone by choice.

My world view became exposed for what it was: a cop-out from facing the realities of life. A coral colony is perhaps a comforting model for the afterlife but does not help with handling the demands of existence while we are alive. The polyp is not only humble, but solitary. Man can aspire to die like a polyp, but must not live like one. For all its unsavoriness, life raises intimacy needs and grants rewards that must not be given up.

I had lived too long, and yet not enough. It was time to start living again.

4

I was almost grateful when there was a soft knock on my room door. I had finally fallen asleep with my clothes on, so I shook fatigue out of my eyes and opened the door to my grand-nephew who had come to fetch me.

Carlos was a bit startled when he noticed my wrinkled look. Before he could say anything, I apologized: "Sorry about my appearance. I could not get to sleep until a couple of hours ago. Do you mind waiting a few minutes while I take a shower and tidy myself up?"

His face broke into a smile. "No problem. I've no school today. I'll go down and get us some coffee while you are getting ready."

Twenty minutes later we were sharing some strong coffee and a few guava pastries. "I had forgotten how well people eat here in Miami."

"That's not all you have forgotten."

"Touché" I replied. Then, getting up, I hugged the lad. "Let's start taking care of that. I want to hear your dad bitch about his broken leg."

Matias F. Travieso-Diaz is a Cuban American engineer and lawyer who, having retired from the practice of law, rediscovered the pleasures of creative writing. In addition to fiction in both English and Spanish, he has written papers on issues relating to Cuba and miscellaneous other topics. You can find him at matiastraviesodiaz.com.

Bud's House

Fay L. Loomis

A few weeks before the Fourth of July, I was curled up on my couch, enjoying the soft light of the patio through my sliding doors, ready to go to bed. Shaken by the buzz of the doorbell, I was pulled from my reverie by a woman's voice.

"I'm Bud's wife. I need to talk."

"What the hell?" I mumbled.

Bud had told me his wife was coming back to decide what was hers and what was his. He didn't say anything about her wanting to talk to me.

I pulled in my breath, blew it out. *Might as well get this over with.* I slowly opened the door.

"Come in," I said. "Would you like to sit down?"

She chose a chair close to the door. Words rushed out. "Bud left your letters on the seat of his Porsche. I see he's been fucking you."

I stopped breathing. The constant shuffle of letters

between Bud and me brought joy. *How could she read them? How could he leave them for her to find?* I snapped back to the present. *She's just found out about us.*

"I thought you'd moved away, the two of you were getting a divorce."

"Oh," she said, quiet for a moment. "We never made a decision about that." Her voice revved up. "The son of a bitch has sent almost no money since I left. We're having a hard time making it." She stopped again, then added, "He says his book royalties have dried up."

I blurted, "Ask him to show you his royalty payments." Bud had shared that he was hiding royalty income from her. I didn't think a lot about it at the time. Suddenly, I was furious. He wasn't supporting his kids.

I shut down my feelings, stood up, and walked toward the door. She followed, all blown out, quiet, subdued. As she walked out into the night, I wondered what she looked like. I hadn't turned on the light, seen her face.

I picked up a pillow and screamed into the soft square shape, then collapsed on the couch and sobbed. Familiar grief from my recent divorce flooded through me.

Over the past year, Bud and I had casually met a few times when he attended events and dropped off books to sell at the antique car museum where I was the director.

We connected when mutual friends invited us to a party. I handed Bud a beer. My eyes took in the thick brown hair that needed a cut, his ready smile, and blue eyes that seemed to reach into his soul. I didn't take my eyes off him the rest of the night. We sat in a corner talking, got the short version of our lives out of the way.

Bud was a literature professor at Michigan State University and a car nut. His wife had taken a teaching job and a lover when she and their two kids moved to Seattle. He puttered aimlessly before deciding to get on with his life. He would fix up the house like his wife had wanted, build the hot rod he had been putting together in his head for the past thirty years.

I had suspended my education so my husband could get a Ph.D. A philosophy professor at the same university, he had receded into alcoholism while I earned bachelor and master's degrees. Recently divorced. Our daughter had taken a job as a designer in New York City.

Bud and I moved on to favorite authors, local hiking trails, and other safe subjects. Neither of us spoke of the loneliness that hovered over us like mist on a rainy afternoon.

Our first week we went to a spectacular play at the new Wharton Center for Performing Arts, hiked through deep snow at Rose Lake, had dinner with a couple Bud knew. The evening turned out warm, friendly.

Afterwards, we stood by the edge of the curb, chilled by the wintry air, unable to say good night. "We need to find a warmer place to continue talking," I said. "Why don't you follow me back to my apartment?"

"Love to," Bud said. A big smile spread across his face. "I thought you were never going to ask."

Bud probably thought we were going to jump into bed. After years of silence, I wanted, needed to talk. We finally quit speaking when Bud walked out into the snowy daybreak.

When I woke in the afternoon, a letter from Bud was tucked into my mailbox. Torn pieces of brown gummed paper covered the print on the used envelope.

3/2/83
Dear Kate:
I know a guy in California named Strother MacMinn.
He lives in the house in which he was raised--a
bungalow on a palm-lined street in Pasadena.

He drives a 1950 Jaguar X-120 roadster, and teaches at the Los Angeles Design Center (& writes for <u>Motor Trend</u>, <u>Road & Track</u>, etc). Strother MacMinn. Pasadena. Bungalow. Jag X-120 roadster LA Design Center. Don't the parts seem to add up nicely? I mean, I'd expect a guy w/ a name like that to live in Pasadena and drive a Jag roadster, etc. etc.

You have that same integrated sense. Your name, first and last, fits (much better than Miller!) what you are. I like your clothes, whether high bucks combat fatigues or the russet skirt and vest with embroidery (?). The scarab pin from SF. Royal purple. Fur-lined white coat. The man's hat with snap-brim turned down. Your apartment. Framed posters/ pictures/ photos/pages. Your elegant (& untouchable!) brass bed.

Your hair--feather cut? Long lower lip. Soft voice. Softly assertive. The rounded cheekbones--I think of a line from a poem by John Logan:"Susannah"--"the high formal bones of your face." You sit with your legs tucked under in a variety of ways. You eat an artichoke and arrange the leaves into a nice pattern. Everything seems to fit— except for the damn Toyota--buy a Jag 120 roadster!

Across the lower part of the typed page, Bud scrawled in red ink *God, I am happy!*

Bud's letter captured my heart. I loved his densely stacked words. His effulgent happiness—emphasized in red ink—seeped into my brokenness.

The second week, we met for a hurried lunch at a funky little diner. Like a magician, Bud pulled from his pocket a tiny vase stuffed with flowers, a couple of small model cars, and a miniature book of poetry. He lined them up along the edge of my plastic tray.

"Bud, you are nuts," I said, looking self-consciously around to see who was watching. No one. I loosened up, giggled, and enjoyed the fuss.

The next day, I opened another letter from Bud.

Dear Kate,

I linger over the memory of our various brief meetings, and how things came together so nicely, how the feeling I had (have) for you developed, became intense. We did so much in a week, and I want our relationship to continue in that same exciting way.

I have this thing about the time-space continuum, as per the <u>Alexandria Quartet</u>—we're thrown together in this place, the gods shake us up and roll us like dice, and people are paired in an almost random manner. In the semi-long lives we've led we've met lots of people, so it's not so odd we should meet, and, yet it <u>is</u> odd that we should meet and develop a (brief) relationship and that I, at least, and perhaps you too, should feel so intensely about another. It has been many years since I've felt about a person the way I feel about you.

I love you.

Bud was signed in large blue letters.

In a way, everything had come together nicely, seemed to fit.

Bud phoned to ask me to come to dinner. I nearly died

233

laughing when he called out the directions. "Go to the Chief Okemos sign. Turn left at the garbage can on the corner and drive down a dirt road until you get to the house." Ever after, I smiled as I turned left at the garbage can, something that happened a lot after that first day.

The road ended in a circle in front of the house, a decaying, flat-roofed anachronism plunked down in the middle of Michigan. Ruts carved up the road and forced me to drive slowly no matter how much I anticipated seeing Bud. When it rained, the ruts filled with pools of water that splashed the sides of my car. I enjoyed the drive, anyhow.

By late spring, the leaves on the trees had transformed the road into a shaded tunnel, lined with waist-high grass. Bud didn't believe in mowing. He said that when his kids were little, he rented a mower to cut paths for them to run through. I would have liked to do that, too.

Warm weather also brought random bursts of color from unkempt lilacs, magnolias, tulips, daffodils, and violets. I wandered through the yard filling my arms with sweet-smelling flowers until they could hold no more.

Every time I pulled up to Bud's place, I wondered if I was at a used car lot or junkyard. His favorite, a red 1937 Ford coupe with a cracked windshield, stood next to his wife's malfunctioning Mercedes. Bud's faded blue Porsche was usually tucked into a spot between the front door and the garage which hid a partially built hot rod and a Model A.

The backyard was filled with rusty car parts and pieces of lumber that formed irregular shapes wherever you looked. The clutter was intriguing. I found the whole place fascinating.

Bud loved to cook for me in the peculiarly shaped kitchen that angled off from the living room. I would sit on one of the rickety chairs, my feet pulled up on the seat, taking in rows of spices and cookbooks. Bud never used either. He relied on garlic, onions, and olive oil.

When I offered to help, he said, "I love to watch you watching me cook. I'm having so much fun." I didn't resist. I found Bud's eagerness to cook and share food refreshing.

During the years I was married, I had prepared many meals. Toward the end of our relationship, the TV had usurped my husband's presence at the dinner table. When he came home, he would settle in front of the TV, read the newspaper, watch the news, and drink beer until bedtime.

A dry sink with an etched glass front was edged into a corner of Bud's kitchen. Stacks of papers and a typewriter covered the round oak table that filled the center of the room. Bud hurried about chopping and stirring. He might halt to show me a paper from one of his students or read something from a publisher. Sometimes letters from his wife rested on top of the piles. I hated to see them because I felt her eyes staring at me. Bud said I could read them. I never did.

By the time the food was ready, Bud had pushed an opening into the midst of the clutter and set two places with an odd assortment of dishes and silverware. With one last flourish, he would rummage up candles, adding coziness to the kitchen.

Bud sensed I was nervous about sex and proceeded slowly. When he slipped his hand into the back of my jeans and caressed my bare skin, I shivered, didn't pull away. He moved his hands toward my breasts. "Not yet," I said.

"OK. I can wait. You're worth waiting for."

We eventually got to the bedroom. Bud let me know how much he appreciated sex. I appreciated his sweetness, gentle touch, and warm body. I was still locked in the past, unable to dissolve into a passionate relationship.

Bud's bed looked like it belonged to a teenage kid. Large undulating curves cut into the honey colored wood of the rope bed which was heaped with an afghan, comforter, and every blanket he owned. A blow-up photograph of Bud's face perched on the dresser at the foot of the bed. Cobwebs floated from the ceiling. A cheap pair of curtains with large flowers hung across the windows that faced into the woods at the edge of the backyard.

I always pulled the curtains back when I was there. I loved to see the morning sunlight and the soft glow of light in the evening. When I asked Bud if I could open the curtains, he said, "Of course. I see how happy it makes you. That makes me happy, too." I soaked up the simplicity of his words, felt cared for.

The bed was a wonder-filled spot for drinking wine and listening to the radio. We especially liked *Prairie Home Companion* on Saturday nights. Whole weekends slipped by, talking, tangled together in that bed.

Bud painted the walls in the nearby bathroom a bright clean purple. He probably did it for me. That's my favorite color. He could have done it to head off negative reactions to his neglected house. He didn't do anything to the cruddy fixtures, the cracked linoleum floor, or the toilet that sprayed water if you leaned ever so slightly to the right—a mystery I found both joltingly funny and annoying.

Bud preferred the bathroom at the end of the hall, his favorite room. "Come look at my new shower curtain. Just found it at Meijer Thrifty Acres for $2.98." His delight prodded me to ignore the rusty shower stall hidden by the clear blue sheet of plastic.

I found the worn red plaid couch in the living room ugly. I was impressed with the rest of the sturdy pine furniture, charged with character that took over the rest of the space. "My wife discovered and refinished each piece," Bud said. "That's a Morris chair, you know." I didn't know and admired the boxy tilt-back chair all the more.

I fell in love with the fieldstone fireplace and slate hearth. Bud got a kick out of me lugging heavy logs through the side door and building rip-roaring fires.

"Hey, you don't need to do that. Let me."

"Yes, I do. Bringing in wood is fun," I said. "I love the fires, the hours we spend in front of the fireplace." We'd lie on a blanket, sip wine and talked while the flames made gigantic flickering shadows on the ceiling. Sometimes we listened to classical music on the radio.

"Why didn't I ever think to do this?" Bud asked.

"I don't know," I said. "We both fell into a vacuum of loneliness. I'm glad we've found some joy."

"Me, too. After my wife left, I was in limbo, just trying to get through those months. I needed desperately to meet someone like you."

"I like the idea of being together, making each other happy," I said, nestling deeper into Bud's embrace. I was at peace.

The memory of words Bud had written about time pushed into my consciousness.

Back back in time which circles, spirals inward like a conch shell of memory, an echo chamber, two threads that unfold in parallel but separate lines until, far in the future, they converge, meet. How odd!

"I'm thinking about how you described our meeting as two lines coming together. The idea has seeped into my brain, sings of the mystery of why two people meet," I said.

"Yes, two lines that have come together," Bud said. Will we ever know why?"

"Do we really know anything?" I responded.

"Nevertheless, if someone said we shouldn't be together, I would swear on a stack of bibles they were wrong."

"Me, too. I know we're supposed to be together. I'm glad we are."

The next day, we took a walk through the pines in back of Bud's house. When we circled back to the shed, Bud surprised me by saying, "I want you to live with me."

"I enjoy our time together, but I can't live here with the unresolved presence of your wife lingering about." In my heart I knew Bud was never going to fix up the place; I could never live there.

Bud was stunned, didn't speak. He finally said, "I'm not going to give up. I'll keep asking."

"What I'd like right now is to see the shed. Can we?" Bud had described his hidey-hole many times, though never offered to take me inside. Now seemed the perfect time.

Bud welcomed the shift. He grinned, pulled a handful of keys from his pocket, and opened the padlock. Boxes of books, magazines, and envelopes stuffed with research notes suffocated the room. Scattered about were writing awards, trophies, report cards, and photos of his wife and children.

A collection of miniature cars rested on top of a bookcase. "The kids broke most of them when they were little. I like to remember that time," he said, melancholy creeping into his voice. "When warm weather comes, I move my typewriter out here and live for the summer."

Bud and I had planned to go to the Fourth of July celebration. His wife's return obliterated that possibility. I went alone and cried through the band concert and the fireworks.

I didn't hear anything from Bud the rest of the summer. I hated being alone, feeling lost, unsure how to crawl out of this hole a second time.

I ran into Bud on the street in the fall. "I've been

following you for the last few blocks, afraid to speak to you." he said. He hurried his words. "After my wife went back to Seattle, I sent you some letters, called. You don't answer. I want to talk to you. I'm so sorry my wife barged into your apartment. I miss you. I love you. I want to be with you."

"You betrayed me," I said in a flat voice. "Left my letters for your wife to find."

Bud's face paled. He pressed on, unable to hold back. "My wife hung around for a few months, told me what an asshole I was, before taking most of the furniture to the West Coast. I'm thinking of going there for Christmas."

He stopped, then picked up his words again. "Why don't you come out to the house and see how it looks without furniture?"

"I'm not going to let you betray me again."

I circled around him and started down the block, then turned back, hurled words at him. "Besides . . . I'm not interested in an empty house."

Fay L. Loomis leads a quiet life in the woods in Kerhonkson, New York. A member of the Stone Ridge Library Writers and the Rat's Ass Review Workshop, her poetry and prose appeared most recently in *Spillwords, Pleiades: Literature in Context, Lothlorien Poetry Journal, Rats Ass Review, The Passionfruit Review, Vita & the Woolf, October Hill Magazine, Loch Raven Review, The Milk House* and *Sunlit Wildness*, a micro-chap, published by Origami Poems Project. Fay's poems are included in five anthologies.